He stood at the door staring at her with an inexplicable look of accusation in his eyes.

Holly lifted her chin slightly. "If you've come here to explain yourself, I don't want to talk to you. If you're any kind of a gentleman, you'll leave right now."

Daniel spoke distinctly, with a sinister pause between each word. "I never said I was a gentleman." Holly caught her breath and held it.

His tone slid into sarcasm. "Gentlemen are supposed to be kind, generous souls with impeccable manners and the purest of thoughts, like your precious Robert! Well, frankly, I think I like your image of me much better—cruel, hard, self-serving." He took a deep breath and brought his voice under control. "And if that's what you think I am, then that's what I'll be."

MELINDA CROSS would love her readers to believe she was kidnapped as a child by an obscure nomadic tribe and rescued by a dashing adventurer. Actually, she is a wonderfully imaginative American writer who is married to a true romantic. Every spring, without fail, when the apple orchard blooms, her husband gathers a blanket, glasses and wine and leads Melinda out to enjoy the fragrant night air. Romantic fantasy? Nonsense, she says. This is the stuff of real life.

Books by Melinda Cross

HARLEQUIN PRESENTS
847—LION OF DARKNESS
889—A VERY PRIVATE LOVE
914—WHAT'S RIGHT
959—THE CALL OF HOME

Don't miss any of our special offers. Write to us at the following address for information on our newest releases.

Harlequin Reader Service
901 Fuhrmann Blvd., P.O. Box 1397, Buffalo, NY 14240
Canadian address: P.O. Box 603,
Fort Erie, Ont. L2A 5X3

MELINDA CROSS

one hour of magic

Harlequin Books

TORONTO • NEW YORK • LONDON
AMSTERDAM • PARIS • SYDNEY • HAMBURG
STOCKHOLM • ATHENS • TOKYO • MILAN

Harlequin Presents first edition December 1989
ISBN 0-373-11224-6

Original hardcover edition published in 1988
by Mills & Boon Limited

CHAPTER ONE

HOLLY SHERWOOD stood at the corner with her shoulders hunched against the icy wind, glaring at the traffic light, willing it to change. The cold wasn't so bad if you kept moving, but this prolonged immobility at every cross-street was a frigid nightmare. It had been the coldest November in New York City's history and, if its first day was a sample, December promised to be worse.

Come on, come on, she willed the light, sharing the sentiments of the dozens of other people crowded around her, all just as anxious as she was to be moving again.

She was as foolishly dressed as most of the other fashion-conscious women in the stalled crowd, with a fawn-coloured cape billowing around her legs and a loose, fur-trimmed hood framing her face. She was also freezing to death.

Blasted capes, she grumbled to herself, tugging fiercely at the front gap the wind kept blowing open, silently cursing the designer who had brought the old fashion back into vogue.

Aside from the bright red of windblown cheeks, Holly's face reflected none of her discomfort. She held it as stiffly as she did the rest of her body, her chin tilted up into the wind, giving her an air of haughty resolution. But, close up, her eyes shattered the illusion. Thickly lashed and the deep brown of a forest floor, they reflected a great sadness; the kind of eyes that inspired heartfelt sympathy with a glance. It frustrated her that she could control precisely the appearance of every other part of her body, that she could conceal her sorrow in every single feature, save that one.

There should have been at least a little warmth generated by the bodies massed around her. Robert certainly would have thought so, but then, the cold had never seemed to affect him—not as long as there was a stranger to meet or a new friend to be made. The lips she'd been holding in a determined line curved slightly as she imagined what he would do if he were here. Scare half these people to death, probably; generating spiritual warmth where the real thing was absent, clapping shoulders, introducing himself, disconcerting the wary by grabbing their stiff hands and shaking them nearly off their shoulders. She chuckled a little and shook her head. He'd been so obsessed with meeting people, making a friend of every stranger, as if he'd know all along he wouldn't have as much time as the rest of them.

Holly glanced at the cold, closed faces around her and sighed. God, she missed him. Still.

At last the red light flashed to green, and, with the impatient precision of a well-trained drill team, the crowd surged forward to cross the street.

She caught a glimpse of her own reflection in a store window as she hurried past, saw a flash of the sorrow that others always saw, and turned her head quickly, disturbed by it. She pulled her hood further forward, as if to hide the face she didn't like much any more, because Robert wouldn't have liked it. That was his greatest flaw, and certainly his greatest charm. Robert Chesterfield had never been able to accept any human emotion that wasn't uplifting. Depression, disappointment, sorrow— none of these had a place in his life, or in his world, for that matter. Life was too short for any of them, he'd said often, and as it turned out he had been perfectly right. He would have hated her grief.

She stomped on down the pavement un- reasonably angry at Robert for dying, for leaving her alone. It was unhealthy to be so furious with a dead man, but it was easier than missing him. Besides, she didn't have anyone else to blame. He'd been alone in his car when he'd fallen asleep and crashed through that guard-rail a year ago, as solely responsible for his own death as he had been for his own life. Damn him, anyway.

The twenty-storey newspaper building seemed squat and ugly amid the surrounding towers of glass and steel, but she had met and worked with Robert there, and so she loved the place. More than the old brownstone she'd lived in for years, this building was home. Good thing, too, she reminded herself. The brownstone was scheduled for renovation shortly after Christmas, and she hadn't found temporary living quarters yet. If something didn't break soon, she'd end up sleeping in one of the newspaper's stock-rooms.

'Holly!' Hampton was waiting when she got out
of the lift on the fifth floor, and before she could
return his greeting he had her crushed against his
barrel chest.

Five years ago, when she'd first come to work
for this rotound, kindly man, she had backed away
from his effusive demonstrativeness, but now his
hug felt good, and she returned it in equal measure.
Hampton was family, as was his wife, Jeanine.
They'd filled in the gap when her own parents had
died, and jumped at the smallest excuse to display
the familial affection they knew she didn't get
anywhere else. He smelled faintly of cherry-blend
pipe tobacco, an aroma she had come to equate
with the man, and like almost as much.

'Hi, Hampton,' she grinned up at him, thinking
what a good Santa Claus he would make with that
round face and ready smile. 'How was your
weekend?'

'Productive,' he said mysteriously, grabbing her
hand and pulling her towards the big double doors
opposite the lifts.

Holly inhaled deeply of the mixed odours of ink
and glue as they passed through a large room filled
with desks, drawing-boards, and the noisy clatter
of headlining machines. Hampton barked orders to
half a dozen men and woman hunched over their
work as he pulled Holly past her own desk towards
the glass-enclosed cubicle that was his office.

'Sit down,' he told her once he had closed the
door behind them. Holly took a seat facing him
across a towering pile of clutter. Rumour had it

that Hampton Phillips hid a desk under all that debris, but no one had ever been able to prove it. 'Since you're being ridiculously stubborn about moving in with Jeanine and me, I think I've found you another place to live until your brownstone is finished.'

She smiled and pushed her hood back, shaking a long sweep of chestnut hair on to her shoulders. 'I love you both for offering, Hampton, but like I told you, I absolutely refuse to be third wheel in a newly-wed love-nest.'

Hampton rolled his eyes, but couldn't suppress the smile. He and Jeanine were hardly newly-weds—they'd been married for twenty-seven years—but their open affection was almost legendary, and Holly worried about intruding on their privacy. 'You're being silly about that, you know—we'd love to have you—but since you turned us down, I have another option for you.' He hesitated for a moment, frowning. 'Trouble is, a job goes with the quarters. You wouldn't be working for me any more.'

'Then forget it,' Holly said instantly, straightening in her chair.

'Now hold on!' He raised a plump hand and looked at her kindly. 'I know you don't want to leave here, any more than I want you to, but it's time, Holly. You're just too good a layout artist to waste on grocery store inserts for the Sunday edition. It's time, way past time, that you moved on to something a little more challenging.'

She pursed her lips stubbornly, not wanting to

move on, not wanting to move anywhere away from the security of Hampton's presence.

Hampton shook his head at her expression. 'Look at you. Here I am, about to offer you the chance of a lifetime, and there you sit, pouting like a spoiled brat on the verge of a tantrum! Now tuck in that lower lip before you trip on it, and hear me out. You know the Chesterfield name, of course . . .'

The sound of Holly's sharp intake of breath stopped him in mid-sentence. He paled instantly, cursing himself for his stupidity. 'Oh, hell! I'm sorry, honey. I didn't mean Robert. I meant his brother, Daniel.'

Holly sat perfectly still in her chair, her back rigid, lower lip tucked in, wondering why it still hurt to hear his name aloud. 'It's not your fault, Hampton.' She tried to make her voice light, but it only sounded shallow. 'I shouldn't be this sensitive after all this time. It's the Christmas season, I think.'

He nodded sympathetically. 'They say the first anniversary of a death is the hardest. It'll get better, Holly, with time.'

She tried to relax and forced a game smile. 'You were talking about Daniel?'

Hampton dragged both hands down his face, making his eyes sag. 'You never met him, did you?'

She shook her head. 'No. Robert kept putting off the family introductions. I don't think there was much brotherly love between them. Maybe I would have met him at the wedding, if we'd had a chance to get that far. Not before.'

'Robert never talked about him?'

'Never.'

'But you read Daniel's column, of course.'

She smiled thinly. 'Like everybody else in the country. How many papers carry it now?'

Hampton frowned and started ticking off a mental count on his fingers while Holly called to mind the little she knew about Robert's brother.

He was the paper's pampered darling, easily responsible for half their circulation, and apparently well aware of the power that gave him. He hadn't seen fit to set foot inside the offices for years, and the weekly column he sent by messenger always appeared unedited, no matter what its content. While his was perhaps one of the best recognised names in American journalism, and while no public figure escaped the cynical lash of his pen, he himself managed to avoid media attention very successfully. Few people would recognise his face on the street, Holly included, and the one and only thing that had ever sent Robert into a stony silence was mention of his brother's name. That hadn't really surprised her. In their writing, at least, the two men had been opposites. Robert's human interest stories had always seen the best of mankind; Daniel's column saw the worst. A philosophical difference that basic rarely encouraged closeness.

'Over two hundred,' Hampton said suddenly.

'What?'

'Over two hundred newspapers carry his daily

column. He's a famous man, Holly. Working for him could be a real feather in your cap, and he's looking for an assistant.'

'That's the job?' she asked incredulously. 'Working for Robert's brother? The prince of darkness himself?'

Hampton made a face at the label pinned on Daniel years before by a corrupt politician he'd exposed. 'He's not as sinister as all that, Holly, and he happens to be a friend of mine.'

Her head tipped in surprise. 'You never mentioned knowing Robert's brother.'

He shrugged, avoiding her eyes. 'It never came up.'

Holly backed off a bit. 'Well, friend or not, Hampton, Daniel Chesterfield works alone. Even I know that. What possible use could he have for a woman who does ad layouts?

Hampton shook his head in exasperation. 'You're selling yourself short again. Forget the advertising part of it. What you do best, what you have an eye for, is looking at a blank page and visualising where pictures and copy should go, and what they should say to have the most impact. It's a gift, and that's what's going to get you the job with Daniel.'

She tossed her hair back from her shoulders in a nervous gesture. 'What job? He doesn't use pictures in his column. What does he need a layout artist for?'

Hampton tapped a pencil against his teeth. 'He started something a little different last year. A new project.'

'Oh?'

'A book, actually. Well, more of a photographic essay . . . about motherhood.'

Holly barked a laugh before she could stop herself. 'Oh, come on, Hampton! What does Daniel Chesterfield know about motherhood—about any human relationship, for that matter? He's a self-proclaimed loner; the man who wrote that love is the irrational delusion of an insecure mind, or some such drivel. Remember?'

Hampton chuckled, remembering the fiery reader response to *that* column—Daniel's Valentine's Day special. 'Maybe that's why he needs help with this particular project. Maybe he doesn't think he has the . . .'

'Humanity?' Holly finished his sentence, one brow arched.

'No, not humanity,' Hampton shot back, irritated. 'Emotionalism is a better word, if it's a word at all. Daniel doesn't express emotions very well, and this is an emotional topic.'

'Then why did he choose it? War, murder, corruption—those are his forte. He does them very well. Why the sudden shift to something he knows nothing about?'

'For reasons of his own.' Hampton's voice was stern. 'And if you're lucky enough to work with him, maybe he'll see fit to tell you what they are.' He hesitated for a moment, watching her face. 'Robert was working with him on this.'

Her lips parted in surprise. Robert was working

on a book with his brother, and never even told her? Why? They told each other everything . . . at least, she'd thought they did.

Hampton went on, pretending not to notice her reaction. 'Daniel needed Robert for this book—needed that talent Robert had for knowing what touched people. And now he needs someone to take Robert's place. He's been stalled on the project for almost a year. I guess he just wasn't ready to face it again, until now.'

Her brows twitched slightly. So. Whether they had been publicly friendly or not, Daniel had obviously been deeply affected by his brother's death, unable to continue alone with a project they had begun together. That, at least, spoke well of him.

Perhaps he wasn't as heartless as he would have everyone believe, and perhaps they could share their common grief, lessening it somehow. How wonderful it would be to work with someone who knew Robert, who missed him—maybe there would even be some comfort in that. 'You said it was a live-in job?'

He nodded. 'Big place, out on Long Island. If you can stand servants and luxury and not fighting traffic on the way to work every morning, it would be a perfect place to wait out the construction on your brownstone. I've already told him about you, shown him some of the work you've done for us, and he's impressed, as much as it's possible for Daniel to be impressed. If you're interested, he'd like you to meet him at his house tonight. So what do you say, Holly?'

'I'm interested,' she replied quietly.

CHAPTER TWO

HOLLY'S obviously middle-class, compact car seemed every bit as intimidated by the Long Island suburb of Brownberry as Holly was herself. It coughed and stalled twice as it crept slowly down Montrose Avenue, as if it knew perfectly well it didn't belong in this neighbourhood of Bentleys and Rolls-Royces.

Most of the homes were set well back from the road, some barely visible through the dense growth of snow-covered shrubbery. If there had not been numbered gateposts at the end of each drive, she would have passed many houses without even knowing they were there.

She followed the lazy twists of the deserted, lamplit road, finally turning into a narrow, snow-dusted drive that curved gently up a small rise. There was a spattering of lights ahead in the distance, winking through the heavily laden boughs of towering white pines.

For all its great size, the Chesterfield house accomplished the illusion of modesty, at least. Carefully placed outdoor lighting cast a golden glow on unadorned red brick, and bright white shutters framed every multi-paned window. There were two large wings off to either side of the central structure, but even they were set back, as if apologising for their excess. It was a beautiful house in a beautiful setting, and she wondered why Robert had been so reluctant to bring her here, insisting instead that they spend all their time together in the city.

The door snapped open before she had a chance to touch the bell, and she looked up with surprise into a face so quietly threatening that it took all her will-power not to run from it. There was no doubt that this was Daniel Chesterfield—his countenance was a perfect reflection of the bitterness that spilled from his mind into every word he wrote—but that he had been related to Robert seemed suddenly, completely impossible.

'So. You were Robert's woman.' She flinched at the label. 'Come in, Ms Sherwood.' It was the unmistakable command of a man who expected to be obeyed. Instantly.

Holly slipped through the door quickly, then jumped when he slammed it behind her.

'Give me your coat, or cape, or whatever it is.'

She remained motionless, staring up at him with her lips slightly parted. This couldn't be Robert's brother. The lack of family resemblance was simply too marked. Robert had been a sunrise compared to this man's brooding darkness. It wasn't cold in the entryway, but she shivered.

She would never have expected that a coldness of spirit could be so visible in a man's eyes; but there it was, in his. They were an unnatural shade of blue, so dark that it looked as if nature had thought to make them black, then changed her mind at the last moment. Part of her wanted to turn her back on that cold stare, and part of her, preposterously, felt impelled to reach out to give some sort of comfort. There was something terribly sad about eyes that empty.

His lips twitched with impatience. 'If you're waiting for me to help you off with your coat, you'll grow old where you stand. Anyone who hopes to work for me has to learn to dress and undress without help.'

She felt her jaw sag involuntarily, and closed it with an audible snap. The flash of sympathy she'd felt dissolved instantly, and she shrugged out of her cape and handed it to him without a word.

He inspected her with almost insulting indifference, his eyes running quickly up and down the length of her body. She bristled a little at his rudeness, brushing at the front of her long green skirt, straightening her shoulders under the matching sweater.

He tossed her cape carelessly on a nearby bench and turned to walk down the wide central hallway of the house. 'Follow me,' he commanded over his shoulder.

She refused to trot behind like an obedient puppy trying to keep up, so she was well behind him when he turned into a wide doorway on the left.

'This is the library,' he said unnecessarily as she followed him down two shallow steps into a room as large as the entire first floor of her brownstone.

A cheery fire crackled and spat behind a screen on the end wall, flanked by two large windows, but, other than that, every inch of wall space was taken up by bookshelves that towered to the ceiling. Desks, armchairs and library tables were scattered in haphazard fashion throughtout the room, each piled high with paper clutter that rivalled even Hampton's disorganised office. But over the mantle directly in her line of sight from the doorway, hung a large oil of the most beautiful woman Holly had ever seen. She was dark, like Chesterfield himself, but her face was warmed by a smile that spoke directly to the heart.

He followed her gaze, then turned abruptly away and walked to a small mahogany bar tucked into one corner. Holly stifled the impulse to ask him who the woman was.

'Sit down,' he said brusquely, busying himself with decanter and glasses. 'Over by the fireplace.'

There was a coldness in his voice that made it perfectly clear she had not made a favourable impression up to this point, and in all likelihood would never see this room again. For some reason, knowing that she had already lost her chance for the job made her relax, and she decided to enjoy the short time she would have here. At least she could tell her grandchildren, should she ever have any, that once she had shared a drink and a fire with the infamous Daniel Chesterfield.

She leaned back in one of the leather wing chairs facing the fire, and regretted for an instant that she would not be spending more time here. As large as the room was, it was still inviting, especially with that woman smiling down from above the mantel, as if approving everything she saw. It would have been a nice place to spend the winter.

'Here you are.' He handed her a beautifully blown snifter that cradled an inch of warm, crystalline brown, then took a seat in the matching chair facing hers. 'I hope you like brandy. It's an evening tradition of mine.'

Holly nodded her thanks, savoured the bouquet, and then the smooth taste of what was undoubtedly a priceless vintage.

This is what you're supposed to do on an evening in December, she mused. Sit in front of a library fireplace, sip warm brandy, and try to read the expression in another pair of eyes. The thought made her realise she was staring at him, but, since he was staring right back, it seemed appropriate. Besides, all she was really doing was comparing him to Robert; there was nothing wrong with that.

Robert had been blond, with crinkles of laughter at the corner of bright blue eyes and a warm, open face that seemed to embody light and gaiety. The man who sat silently opposite her now, measuring her, was none of those things.

The firelight sharpened the angles of his face, and she smiled at the sudden thought that he looked every bit as fierce as one might have expected from reading his column. He had the hungry look of all reporters she had met, except Robert, but his was even more savage, intensifield by the keen intelligence that shone from his eyes. His hair was as black as his eyes should have been, long enough to curl over the collar of his white sweater, unruly enough to cross his brow whenever he turned his head too quickly.

A hundred years ago a woman would have been afraid of a man who looked like he does, she thought. He would have been a pirate, or a renegade, or, at the very least, the kind of man who made other men want to lock up their wives and daughters. Forget the physical features—you don't have to look any further than the eyes to see the ruthlessness hiding there, just beneath the veneer of civilisation.

'Well, Ms Sherwood?' He interrupted her inspection before she got any further. 'Would you like a photograph to study at your leisure, or are you just about finished?'

There was absolutely no amusement in his tone, but she laughed anyway. 'If that's all the time I get, I'd better opt for the photograph. I'm not nearly finished. You have an interesting face, Mr Chesterfield.'

For a moment he looked as though he might smile, then apparently thought better of it and turned his face towards the fire. 'We didn't look at all alike.'

It unnerved her a little, that he had known what she was thinking. 'No. You certainly didn't.'

He nodded without looking at her, steepling his fingers under his chin. 'Since you're here, you're obviously interested in working for me. Did Hampton tell you about the book?'

'Briefly.'

'Good. There's a series of photos in the folder on the table next to you. Examine them, then tell me how you'd use them in a layout.'

Holly exchanged her glass for the folder on the table, opened it, and was immediately captivated by the four photographs inside. Three of them were full-face shots of a beautiful, but badly undernourished child. Enormous, sorrowful brown eyes looked out at her from a pathetically thin face. The fourth shot showed the same child in profile, gazing up at the weary smile of a woman who was obviously his mother. The first three photos showed clearly the pain of poverty and hunger, as did the fourth; yet the facial expression of the child and mother as they looked at each other somehow dispelled the horror one knew existed behind the pictures. The line of love from one set of eyes to the other was so visible, so overpowering, that it became a silent statement of triumph.

'Oh, my!' Holly whispered, sinking immediately to her knees on the floor in front of the fire, shuffling the photos before her, completely forgetting Chesterfield's presence. Within seconds she had the photographs arranged, then remembered why she had done it. She looked up to find him leaning forward in his chair, arms draped across his knees, staring down at the pictures.

'Are you finished?'

'Yes.' She looked back at the photos and sighed, then gestured at the two she had turned upside-down. 'These are good, but redundant. This one, with the child on the verge of tears, that's the one to use. All alone on a field of white, with the picture showing the child and mother together on the facing page. There is no other way.'

'And where would you put the captions?'

'In the waste basket,' she said firmly. 'These pictures don't need captions. Good ones never do. Who took them?'

He gathered up the photos and slipped them back into the folder. 'I did.'

'You?' She climbed back into her chair, staring at him with disbelief.

'Why should that surprise you? I'm a reasonably intelligent man, perfectly capable of pushing a button on a camera.'

She frowned at him, trying to see what lay behind his eyes. 'Yes, of course you are,' she replied softly, thinking that there was a depth of feeling in those shots one would never expect from the man who wrote Daniel Chesterfield's column.

He turned away from her inspection. 'When can you move in?' he asked abruptly.

'What?' she breathed, suddenly wanting this job very much, wanting the opportunity to work with photographs this exquisite, a subject this moving.

'The position is yours, if you want it, Ms Sherwood. When can you move in? Tomorrow?'

She felt her whole face lift with the force of her smile. 'Yes. Of course.'

'Good. Come along and I'll show you the guest-house. You can stay in the main house, if you like, but Hampton gave me the impression that you valued your privacy. Besides, you'll probably need a place to retreat occasionally. I'm not an easy man to work for.'

Holly followed him back to the front door in a happy daze. She had come prepared to sacrifice privacy in exchange for a place to live for the next several months; prepared to find an occasional moment of limited solitude in a single room, at best. She had never expected a home of her own, and the prospect cheered her enormously.

She was so distracted that she tried to slip on her cape backwards. 'Oh, dear,' she giggled when she realised what she was doing.

She looked up at him with a childlike smile, but he was leaning against the wall with his arms crossed over his chest, his expression stern. Her smile faded and she looked down and started to fumble with the buttons on her cape.

'Damn,' she muttered under her breath, feeling the blood rush to her face as she struggled with the top button.

'Oh, for heaven's sake,' he said impatiently, snatching her hands away and proceeding to button the cape himself. 'Let me do that, or we'll be here all night.'

She lifted her chin out of the way as he worked the buttons, and tried to control the furious blush of embarrassment by concentrating on his face.

It would be such a handsome face, she mused, if only it weren't so fierce-looking all the time. Like now, with his brows reaching for each other and his lips tightened into a thin line of concentration. Robert had never looked angry like that. Never.

Suddenly the last stubborn button slipped into its proper place, his facial muscles relaxed, and his eyes shifted to hers and stopped. She felt his fingers tighten on the fabric beneath her chin, and then his hands were quiet.

For a split second Holly forgot where she was, who she was, and how to breathe. Her gaze fastened in wide-eyed wonder on his lips, just inches away, and some part of her mind marvelled to see that he had a beautiful, sensual mouth when he wasn't trying to look so stern. When she finally remembered to take a breath, it caught in her throat with a tiny hitch, then escaped her lips in a soft rush of air. The caress of her breath on his face jolted him, caused his head to snap back and his eyes to narrow. They locked on hers with surprise, then a moment of confused wonder, and finally, unmistakable anger. He dropped his hands quickly and turned away.

'We'll go out through the kitchen,' he mumbled gruffly, striding away down the hall.

This time Holly did trot behind him to keep up, licking lips that were suddenly dry. She paid no attention whatsoever to the route they took through the cavernous house. If her life had depended on it, she wouldn't have been able to describe the kitchen they passed through on the way to a rear door. What she could have described, in great detail, was Daniel Chesterfield's back—the interplay of broad shoulder muscles under the thin knit of his white sweater; the angry swing of arms that terminated in clenched fists; the determined stride of a man walking purposefully away from something that made him want to run.

He snatched a parka off a hook by the back door without stopping, and slipped it on as he walked into the snowy night, leaving Holly to close the door behind them.

She stopped just outside and took a deep, cleansing breath of the cold air. She lifted her face to the sky and forced memories of Robert, but the moment she licked a falling snowflake from her lips, she wondered involuntarily what snow would look like on Daniel Chesterfield's black hair. She raced after him to see.

A shovelled path led through the pines that surrounded the house to a cottage that looked like home to Holly the moment she saw it. The feeling was reinforced as soon as she stepped inside and Chesterfield switched on the lights.

'Oh, it's perfect!' she cried, bringing her hands together under her chin.

He closed the door quietly behind them, then just stood there staring at her, his hand still on the knob. 'You've got snow on your hair, and on your eyelashes,' he said. The intimacy of the observation startled her.

She exhaled quickly in a half-laugh, then brushed nervously at her hair as she looked around the room.

There was a small fieldstone fireplace, a handbraided rug over the gloss of a planked floor, and a casual grouping of furniture that invited informality.

'It was never intended to be someone's home,' he said uncertainly, as if he'd just remembered that one of them should say something. 'It's really very small . . .'

'No, no, it's a perfect size. I love it.' She swept through the cosy room, touching a lamp here, a table there, taking possession.

Chesterfield crossed his arms over his chest and watched the ritual with narrowed eyes. 'The bedroom and bath are through that door,' he nodded to the left, 'and the kitchen, such as it is, is right on the other side of that snack bar. We can have all the furniture put in storage if you'd like to bring your own things.'

'No,' she said thoughtfully. Then, spinning to face him, her eyes alight, she repeated, 'No. I like it just the way it is. I'll put my furniture in storage instead, if you don't mind.'

'Whatever,' he shrugged, tearing his eyes from hers and looking up at the ceiling with a pretence of interest.

I want to touch him, she realised with a start, feeling her hand twitch with the unfinished gesture. Embarrassment that the thought had even crossed her mind made her turn away. She kept looking around the room, seeing the same objects again and again, until it struck her that she was trying not to look back at him.

This is ridiculous, she told herself. He's your employer now. You're not going to be able to avoid looking at him for ever, so you'd better get used to it. Besides, what are you afraid of?

She forced her eyes to his, then jerked them away quickly. 'Can you tell me something about the job?' she asked, plucking nervously at a loose thread on the back of the couch next to her.

'Of course. Sit down, or would you rather go back to the main house?'

'No, no. This is fine.' She almost ran around to the front of the couch and sat stiffly on the edge, her hands clutched together in her lap.

He sat in an adjacent chair, looked at her once, then turned to study the empty grate. His hair was still glistening from the short walk outside, and Holly felt a stab of regret that she hadn't seen the snowflakes sprinkled on that field of black before they'd melted.

'I go out on Mondays,' he began, 'and Tuesdays I devote to my columns for the week, so those days will be yours, to spend however you like. The rest of the week, Saturday and Sunday included, I work on the book—and I ought to warn you, once I start, it's hard to stop. I work through the night, when things are going well.' He brushed a shock of hair from his forehead in an impatient, unconscious gesture he obviously made often. 'We'll have to work closely together until you see where I'm going with this project. After that, you might be able to handle some of the layout on your own. Did Hampton tell you exactly what I was looking for?'

Hampton told me you couldn't express emotion,

she remembered suddenly, staring into eyes that seemed almost navy blue in this light. She came to herself with a start and looked down at her hands. 'Not really,' she answered after a silence that had been too long. 'Just that you needed someone with an eye for layout. Where to put the pictures and the copy—that sort of thing.'

He pursed his lips and nodded. 'Well, you're certainly capable of that, but so are a thousand other people in New York City. I need more. I need . . .' He wiped one hand across his face in frustration as he searched his mind for the right words. 'I need someone who can curb my tendency to turn everything into hard news and dry facts; someone who can sense instinctively what it takes to touch people.' His chuckle was bitter. 'Robert was very good at that. I'm not, I'm afraid.'

He tilted his head sideways to eye her, and she saw a self-deprecating smile touch and lift one side of his mouth for only an instant. 'Well, what do you think, Ms Sherwood? If I supply the photographs, can you supply the heart?'

The question was so plaintive that she had to blink twice before answering. 'It's very important to you, isn't it? That this book will reach out and touch people?'

He glared at her as if he hated her for asking that question, and she wondered if he always reacted with anger to anything that stirred emotions he preferred to keep hidden.

'Yes,' he said flatly.

'I'd like to try,' she said quietly. 'Very much.'

'Even though it will mean living here, working closely with me?' There was a subtle shift in the timbre of his voice that sounded almost like a threat.

'Having to live in is one of the best parts of this job,' she said carefully. 'Didn't Hampton mention the construction on my brownstone?'

'Yes, yes, I know all that. I just thought you might find the situation awkward because of . . . the relationship you had with Robert.'

'To tell you the truth,' she smiled, a little bemused, 'it almost seems as though he's still alive, still watching over me, making sure everything turns out all right . . .'

'Oh, *please.*'

Her smile vanished.

'Spare me the eulogy. I heard enough about wonderful, warm, loving Robert when he was still alive. It was nauseating then. Hearing him get credit for good deeds after his death is almost more than I can stomach. Besides, that wasn't what I meant. What I really wanted to know is if you could stand working with someone who hated the man you loved.'

Holly gaped at him. 'Hated? You hated Robert? Your own brother?'

'Almost as much as he hated me,' he replied, his eyes narrowing. 'As a matter of fact, our mutual hatred was the driving force in each of our lives, and if you didn't know that, Ms Sherwood, you didn't know Robert at all.'

She drew in a sharp breath and shivered, as if a

cold wind had just blown through the room. 'I knew you didn't get along,' she said, choosing her words with care, 'but more from what he didn't say than what he did. Robert rarely mentioned you, but I'm sure there was no hatred on his part. Robert loved everyone. He was incapable of hatred.'

His laugh sent a chill up her spine.

'And I don't believe that you hated him, either,' she blundered on stubbornly, refusing to accept what she couldn't understand. 'Maybe that's just your way of dealing with your grief.'

'Grief!' His reaction was startling. He sprang from the chair as if she had slapped him, stood perfectly still for a moment as he faced the fireplace, then turned on her, his face suffused with blood, his hands clenched at his sides. 'I do not grieve for my brother!' he snapped. 'The one and only thing I miss about him is what he was doing for the book. God knows, it was the only useful thing he ever did in his whole life. You're damn lucky he died before you made the mistake of marrying him!'

Holly sat absolutely still, staring up at the embodiment of a rage so blind, so total, that it threatened to consume the man who tried to contain it. His eyes were frightening.

'I can't believe you said that,' she whispered, her lips barely moving.

His mouth was still open from the last word, and now he expelled a long breath through his parted lips. He let his eyes fall closed as he shook his head.

'Neither can I,' he said shakily, but he wasn't apologising for the sentiment, only for the display of temper. 'Believe it or not, exhibitions like that are quite out of character for me.' He tiptoed delicately over the words, but his voice quivered, and Holly could see a prominent vein throbbing on the side of his forehead. He ran a hand back through his hair, leaving a flattened trail through the hedge of black. 'Ms Sherwood—good lord! I've just brought out all the family skeletons for you to look at, and I don't even know your first name. Hampton told me, but I forgot.'

'Holly,' she whispered, still afraid to move.

'Holly,' he repeated dully. 'What a Christmassy name.'

There was obvious derision in the way he said it, and Holly hated him for that. Those had been Robert's precise words the first time they'd met, but when Robert had said them they had sounded quite different . . . almost magical.

'I really should be going, Mr Chesterfield.' She rose from the couch.

'Daniel.'

'Daniel, then. I have a lot to do at home tonight if I intend to move in here tomorrow.'

He stared at her for a moment. 'I'm surprised you're still willing to work with me, after my little demonstration.' He tipped his head in a minor accolade. 'But since you are, I promise I won't subject you to that kind of scene again.'

She tried to smile, but it wavered a little.

He hesitated, his hand on the doorknob, and for

a moment it almost looked as if he would press his forehead against it. 'Listen, Holly. I'm sorry about . . .'

'It doesn't matter. Really.'

'Of course it matters!' For a man who had just promised never to lose his temper again, his face was alarmingly red. He exhaled a deep breath and a strand of hair lifted from his forehead and the flush receded. 'But I think it might be better if we didn't talk about my brother again.'

Holly nodded in silent agreement. So much for shared grief and things in common! And perhaps that was better. Suddenly she was relieved that he didn't look at all like Robert, that she wouldn't be spending every day with a man whose very appearance would only serve to remind her of what she had lost. Yes. This way was much better.

Oddly enough, she was strangely comfortable with him as he walked her around the side of the great house and out to the front drive. The quiet fall of snow seemed to envelop them in peace, and his outburst in the guest-house already seemed like something that had happened long ago, to someone else entirely. Surely this contemplative man was incapable of such seething rage?

He strolled next to her with his head down, hands jammed into his parka pockets, snowflakes catching in the dark strands of his hair and glittering there like sequins.

He opened her car door and braced his arms on its top, looking at her quietly. Maybe things would have turned out differently if he'd only said something—anything—but he just stood there, staring at her as if all the world's secrets were hidden in her eyes. She wasn't certain, but she didn't think anyone had ever looked at her so intently before, so expectantly. She finally spoke to break the silence.

'Thank you for the brandy.'

'You barely touched it.'

'You distracted me with your photographs.' She couldn't make herself look away from his eyes. 'Well,' she said lamely, still staring at him, still motionless, 'I'd better be going.'

Somehow she knew he was going to touch her, and yet it still surprised her. His eyes never left hers as he reached over the door between them and pushed her hair away from her face. His fingers slipped between the silky curls, grazing her cheek. They were so cold that she reached up without thinking to warm them with her own.

He jerked his hand away quickly, frowning. 'Sorry,' he muttered. As he jammed his hands back into his pockets and looked away, she realised that the alien expression he was wearing was embarrassment, but for what? For touching her in the first place? For reaching out to make contact with another human being? She had been like that once, too—before Hampton and Jeanine—before Robert. She remembered the loneliness of self-imposed isolation, and felt her sympathy rise once again as she gazed on this dark, angry, solitary man. She slipped off her glove and extended her hand, meaning only to offer friendship, but the moment her fingers brushed the dark stubble of his cheek, the gesture became something else.

As soon as she touched him the muscle in his jaw tensed under her fingers, then a suspicious frown tugged at his dark brows and nipped at the corners of his eyes. She felt those eyes searching hers, probing with the hostile expression of a man who never expects to see anything good, and therefore never does. His stare was almost an accusation, and for one crazy moment she felt as if her touch had violated him somehow, and that he was about to slap her face. And yet, she couldn't pull her hand away, or her eyes, because they were her only link to this man, and that the link should be broken at this particular moment was unthinkable.

When he finally moved, it was slowly, and with great care. He lifted one hand to press hers more firmly against his cheek, as if he, too, were reluctant to sever that tenuous bond. His other hand slid into the hair at the back of her neck and pulled her firmly forward against the door between them. The most sensuous feeling Holly had ever experienced was the door-handle digging painfully into her thigh.

He never closed his eyes, never freed her from the wordless question they asked until their lips brushed, then touched, then clung briefly in a bittersweet communion that neither one of them fully understood. Suddenly his eyes slammed shut and he drew in a sharp breath, then his lips softened as his head bent into the kiss. He released her hand to cradle her head, pulling her closer, while his mouth worked hers like a violinist stroking an instrument he has never played before. Holly had no chance to think of either responding or resisting, and no conscious will to do either. The first rush of breath that had left her body when she was pulled against the door seemed to drag something else behind it—some hot, frightening sensation that tugged at her stomach and spread upwards. Her lips felt swollen when he finally jerked his head away, and she found it difficult to catch her breath.

'Damn,' he murmured, frowning down at her.

'Damn?' she repeated softly in a question her eyes echoed. For some reason, that made him smile. Her heart lurched as she saw his face free from anger, and all she could think of was how beautiful he was.

'I think it's time you went home, Holly.'

'Yes,' she breathed, sinking into the car seat, taking the weight off legs that were about to buckle anyway.

She started the car and let it warm up as she watched him walk through the snow towards the front door. There was something about the way he turned on the porch to look at her that reminded her of Robert, and she winced at the unexpected flash of guilt.

Stop it, Holly, she told herself firmly. He's been dead for a year; you've mourned for a year; you've been alone for a year. Is it any wonder you responded to a little human warmth?

'I'm sorry, Robert,' she whispered under her

breath as she eased the car into gear. All the way home she tried to picture his face—the bright, laughing blue eyes; the fair hair tumbling totally out of control; the effervescent good will that seemed to radiate from him constantly—but the dark, determined angles of Daniel's face kept superimposing themselves on Robert's image. Her breath quickened in the solitude of the car as she recalled the way he had pulled her towards him.

She frowned, remembering Robert's kisses, wanting the memory to be fraught with the same tension that Daniel's touch had drawn from her. But all she could recall was the incredible sense of peace she had felt in his arms.

'So what's wrong with peace?' she said aloud.

CHAPTER THREE

HOLLY stood in the middle of the guest-house living-room, arms akimbo, looking an empty day right in the eye, a little uncertain what to do with it.

The guest-house sparkled from a recent cleaning, and the faint, pleasant scent of lemon furniture polish still hung in the air. The small bathroom gleamed; crisp fragrant sheets were turned back on the large bed; and the small, utilitarian kitchen had been fully stocked since she'd glanced in the empty cupboards last night.

'Now what do I do?' she asked the empty room, flopping her hands at her sides.

Unpacking had gone too fast. With the guest-house furnished with everything from cutlery to linens, she had marked only clothing and personal items for delivery to the Chesterfield property, and those had been neatly stored in spacious closets and drawers within the first hour. She had used up another hour preparing and eating a rather elaborate luncheon salad, and now found herself with time on her hands. It was a brand new sensation, and Holly found it a little disturbing.

My God, she thought. Time on my hands. When was the last time that had happened? Years ago, certainly; before Mom and Dad died; before

I had to learn to depend on myself for everything.

She spotted a small stack of books she'd brought from home, books she'd never had time to read, and a tiny, astonished smile lifted her lips. She snatched the top one, nearly ran through the bedroom to the bath, and filled the spotless tub with fragrant bubbles. After discarding her clothes in an untidy pile, she pinned her hair on top of her head and sank into the steaming water with her book held high. Thirty minutes later she crawled out, feeling deliciously waterlogged, lethargic, and pleasantly guilty at such an unheard-of midday indulgence.

She cleared a spot on the misty mirror with her fist and made a face at her reflection. What little make-up she had started with this morning had been steamed away in the bath, and with her chestnut hair up and her face still flushed, she looked much younger than her twenty-five years.

She toyed with her hair idly, searching for a more mature look, wondering why wearing it up had never given her the same aura of sophistication it seemed to give other women. It was the eyes, she decided, that sentenced her to a perpetually childlike appearance. They were too large, too widely spaced, implying youthful innocence no matter what their expression. She tried dropping her lids to a vampish half-mast, but that only made her look sleepy. It was one of the things Robert had loved about her.

'You have one of those wonderful faces that always looks brand new,' he'd told her once. 'As if sorrow and hardship had never touched you; as if you'd been born just this morning.'

At the time, the pronouncement had irritated her a little. She *had* had hard times in her life, and struggles, and sorrow, too. She'd paid her dues and, in a way, wanted that to show, if only a little. But Robert had always turned away from faces that told the story of life, pained by the lines old sorrows left behind; and so eventually she learned to be grateful that her own face didn't reflect her past.

She grunted at her reflection, at the faint lines tugging her mouth downward. Those were the new marks of grief, conceived at Robert's death and developed over the past year. He would have hated them.

She sighed and unclipped her hair, letting the luxuriant natural waves fall around her shoulders, then slipped into a white terry robe and padded out to the living-room in her bare feet.

'Hi.'

'Oh!' She jerked like a marionette and automatically pressed a small hand to her heart. 'You scared me to death.'

'Sorry.' Daniel was slumped on the couch, his feet propped up on the coffee-table, his hands locked behind his head.

Holly frowned at him, trying to dispel the fleeting impression of mischief she thought she'd seen in his expression. When she concentrated on his features, she realised how fanciful a notion that had been. Daniel Chesterfield was not the mischievous type.

Now *there* was a face with a history, she thought, intrigued for the moment by the faint indentation over the straight nose that remembered a scowl, unconsciously comparing it to Robert's smooth untroubled brow.

'I knocked. Nobody answered.'

Suddenly she remembered that he had entered her home without permission, and her jaw stiffened slightly. 'So you just walked in?' She stopped before she said 'just like you owned the place', reminding herself that he did.

'Habit. One I'll have to break, I suppose.'

He didn't even have the decency to look sheepish, and that, along with his obvious nonchalance in a situation that made her distinctly uncomfortable, irritated her.

'Well,' she said huffily, 'I'm glad I had the sense to pull on a robe before I came out here.'

'That makes one of us.'

She came within a breath of laughing and shattering her pose of righteous indignation. After all, there was nothing funny about nearly prancing out naked in front of a man she'd known for less than twenty-four hours; and there was certainly nothing funny about his open admission that he would have enjoyed it. Still, the laugh bubbled just beneath the surface, and she had to press her lips tightly together to contain it.

There was something different about him today. Something easier, more relaxed, a lightness of spirit that somehow seemed to invite frivolous behaviour and stifled giggles. He looked perfectly proper, of course, but his eyes seemed a lighter shade of blue than they had last night, and it almost looked as if he were making a concentrated effort not to smile. She guessed correctly that this was a rare frame of mind for him, and she didn't want to shatter it.

Still, there was last night to think about. She had responded to him much too easily, and that was when his mood had been considerably darker. Today he might be even more dangerous.

She tightened her robe's belt with a jerk and started to turn away.

'Don't go.' His tone was half-command, half-plea, and altogether irresistible. 'Here.' He straightened and leaned over to pat the armchair next to the couch. 'Sit with me for a while.'

'I should dress,' she began lamely, but he waved his hand in a remnant of the impatience she had seen last night.

'Don't bother. That thing you've got on must be about as decent a covering as anything you own. You look like a mobile mummy.'

She was about to say that the floor-length robe didn't feel very decent with nothing on underneath, but decided against it. Instead, she curled into the armchair with her feet under her. 'You're very relaxed this afternoon.' She reached for idle conversation.

He leaned forward on the couch and rested his elbows on his knees. His eyes bored into hers from less than two feet away. 'I just finished this weeks's column. I alway get fat and lazy and contented once that's out of the way.'

She tried for a nervous smile, finding it impossible to imagine him as any of those things. He was the kind of man who thrived on pressure-cooker timetables and impossible deadlines.

'And how long will that last?'

He made a wry face without moving his eyes from hers. 'Until tomorrow morning, if I'm lucky. Anna says I'm a good time for one night out of the week, and a write-off for the rest. You look even better without make-up, you know that?'

She swallowed self-consciously. The compliment had been tacked on like an afterthought.

'Anna will get used to you, by the way. Ignore her for the time being, if you can.'

Holly smiled a little and started to play with the hood on her robe with both hands, wanting for some reason to pull it over her head.

'As a matter of fact, having you around will be good for her. Put things back in perspective, maybe.'

She didn't have the slightest idea what he was talking about, but none of it seemed important anyway. What was important was that now he had leaned back on the couch, and was looking at her through half-closed eyes that seemed suddenly predatory. She caught herself twisting a loose thread around one finger, and clasped her hands in her lap to keep from unravelling the whole robe.

There's nothing going on here, she kept telling

herself. You're just having a friendly chat with
your new employer in the middle of the afternoon—in a bathrobe, a little puritan voice
reminded her—and if you're a little tense—well,
that's to be expected. It's not necessarily a reaction
to *him,* just to a day that's been full of change.

She smiled at the logic of that marvellous
rationale. The smile faltered a bit when she realised
all the logic in the world didn't explain her
fluttering pulse or her inability to tear her gaze
from his eyes.

She moved her shoulders inside her robe. 'I
really should get dressed . . .'

The afternoon sun slanted through the window,
highlighting his head as he lifted it slightly. For an
interminably long moment, he stared at her
silently. 'We have to talk, Holly,' he said finally,
and she trembled at all that was left unsaid in that
sentence.

'All right,' she breathed, her eyes wide and wary.

His smile was more an expression of frustrated
bafflement than one of pleasure. 'I don't suppose
there's any point to beating around the bush, is
there? Not after last night.' One deep breath erased
the amusement from his face and steadied his eyes.
The blue was darkening again. 'The simple fact is
that we're physically attracted to each other.
There's nothing wrong with that, of course, as long
as we can manage to work together under those
conditions.'

Holly could feel shocked dismay creeping from
the inside out to plant itself on her face. It wasn't

that he'd said it out loud; it was just that he'd said it so matter-of-factly, so emotionlessly. She felt suddenly cold in the heavy terry robe, and terribly embarrassed.

'Personally,' he went on blithely, 'I think we can handle it if we acknowledge the problem, and deal with it openly. Either we sleep together or we don't, but it should be decided now, so it doesn't interfere with our work.'

Holly's mouth sagged open, then snapped shut as she stared at him in disbelief. Her expression prompted one side of his mouth to twitch. It wasn't quite a smile, but it was close.

'Was that a little too straightforward for you, Holly?'

She dropped her eyes, concentrated for a moment on folding her hands together in her lap, then looked up. 'I'm afraid you've assumed too much,' she said coolly.

'Really?' His tone was mocking, but she refused to give him the satisfaction of a response.

He was behind her chair almost before she was aware of any movement at all; strong, warm hands encircling her neck, fingers reaching down to follow the line of her collarbone under her robe. For a moment the sensation of his hands on her body paralysed her, then she shot forward to leap from the chair. His hands jerked her back, pressing deeply but gently into her flesh, and before she could move again, he bent over her shoulder and touched the side of her neck with his lips.

'In that case, you should probably start fighting

. . . right about now,' he murmured against her skin, sliding one hand deeper into her robe until his fingers slid over the initial rise of her breasts.

At the moment of her startled gasp, he tipped her chin back with one hand and bent quickly to kiss her. Holly kept telling herself to jump from the chair, spin on him, maybe slap his face, and her mind kept saying, 'OK, I'll do that,' but all her body did was arch into the kiss and tremble under his hands, and that response was all the acquiescence he needed. He lifted his head until his mouth was a hair's breadth from hers, blew lightly into her open mouth, then brushed her lips with his once, and then again. Holly felt every muscle in her body tighten in frantic preparation for action she couldn't begin to predict, but at that moment he lifted his head away.

She kept her eyes closed, startled by the sudden sensation of solitude. He no longer hovered over her; his hands were no longer plunging into the secret depths of her robe; she was alone. The ugly process of thought replaced the mindless process of feeling, and she remembered to be embarrassed, shocked by her own behaviour, bewildered that she had allowed such a thing to happen. Never in her life had she been so totally out of control, and her thoughts reeled with what her helplessness under his hands implied. She'd been cold-shouldering eager young men away from her for years, never quite believing that passion was the province of women as well as men, until this moment. Even her responses to Robert had always been . . . well . . .

pure, in a way; and she had loved Robert without reservation. My God! What would Robert have thought if she'd ever behaved like this with *him?* And what did Daniel think, for that matter? Probably that she was an animal. Holly Sherwood, the animal.

The description loomed in her mind like a funhouse grin, and the laughter, the damnable, inappropriate laughter trailed behind it like a fish on a line. She pressed her lips so tightly together that it hurt, stifling a giggle that didn't match the circumstances at all, then leaned forward in her chair and opened her eyes to see him kneeling right in front of her—kneeling, for crying out loud, like some kind of merry supplicant.

She saw his grin and sobered instantly, cocking her head until all her hair fell to one side. 'What are you smiling at?' she demanded, trying to look angry.

'That's the first time a woman I've tried to seduce had to fight to keep from laughing out loud,' he shrugged. 'I don't know how else to react.

'Listen, about that . . .'

He rose slowly to his feet until he towered over her, then bent and braced his hands against the arms of her chair, effectively trapping her. His breath stirred the tendrils of hair curling around her ears and made her shiver. 'I hope you're not going to try to explain away what just happened between us with phases of the moon, or any of that garbage.' He pecked her on the nose, almost playfully, making her flinch. 'Besides, if you insist on pretending there isn't a very real attraction between us, I'm just going to have to prove it all over again.'

She blinked sombrely, acknowledging the warning, and he nodded his approval. He looked very stern as he straightened to his full height, lips compressed and arms folded across his chest, but there was something merry in his eyes.

She pulled the sagging lapels of her robe closely together and cleared her throat. 'It's probably just because you're Robert's brother.'

His gaze sharpened under lowered brows and Holly tensed, ready for another display of temper, but after a moment his features relaxed. His voice was flat when he spoke. 'I see. I look so much like Robert, and act so much like Robert, and apparently kiss so much like Robert, that you responded to me just as you always did to him, is that it?'

She looked away quickly, her brows twitching.

'Did you sleep with him?'

'Sleep with him?' Holly jumped up from her chair and tightened the belt on her robe with a nervous jerk. 'That's none of your business!'

Daniel smiled grimly and followed her with his eyes as she paced back and forth in front of the fireplace. 'No, of course you didn't,' he said disdainfully. 'That wasn't Robert's style, was it? Sex was a little too earthy, a little too human for Robert, because whatever the hell he was, he certainly wasn't human.'

She spun on him with her hand lifted and tears of angry frustration already on her lower lids, but he caught her wrist effortlessly and used it to jerk her against him. She still could have eluded his grasp, turned away, and she would have, if he had done anything, absolutely anything but cradle her face in both hands and tip it gently up towards his.

'It wasn't real, Holly, what you felt for him,' he whispered. 'But this is.' He caught her upper lip delicately between his teeth and touched it with his tongue, eliciting a shudder she couldn't contain. 'This is real, and it's what you want.' Before she could stop him he had one hand inside her robe, under her breast, pushing it up to feel the pounding of her heart.

'No!' she gasped, at last spinning away, clutching the front of her robe, turning to face him only when she was safe distance away. 'All you're talking about is sex! A purely physical attraction, and there was more to Robert than that! He had more than that to give! He changed my life. He made me see the whole world in a different way. He made . . . everything . . . better.' She drew out her last words, staring at him defiantly.

For a long time he made no response at all, and, though he had never taken his eyes from hers, she had the feeling that there was no life behind the eyes at all, that he had gone somewhere she couldn't follow. She couldn't read his expression, wasn't even sure that she wanted to; but she was sure that she wanted to keep looking at it, and that in itself was troubling.

He's a user, she told herself. A hard, bitter man who undoubtedly uses woman like he uses everything else in his life; to fulfil a very specific need. But there's nothing else there. Nothing else he can give you. And his next words confirmed it.

'We'll end up in bed, you know,' he said as casually as another man might remark on the weather. 'Maybe not tonight, or tomorrow, but eventually. I don't think either one of us could prevent that from happening, even if we wanted to.'

This time when she reached inside for indignation, she found it. 'I doubt that,' she said coldly. 'I expect a great deal more from a relationship than that.'

'Fine,' he shrugged, apparently unconcerned. 'We'll get acquainted first. Maybe that will satisfy your naïve expectations of what comprises a relationship between a man and a woman.' He covered the distance between them quickly and took her by the shoulders. His eyes were narrowed and a few strands of black hair fell over his forehead. 'But I'll tell you this. With or without the courting prelude you seem to expect, the attraction you're fighting so damn hard is a rare thing. Maybe even a precious one. It doesn't happen that often.'

Holly expected him to snap her against his chest and kiss her violently, and she was prepared for that, prepared to push him away or scream or beat on him with her fists. But she wasn't prepared for gentleness, for the way he wound his hands into her hair and eased her face towards his, for the way he moved his lips against hers so softly, so tenderly, that she felt more like she was being savoured than simply kissed. She wasn't prepared for that at all.

She took the first shaky breath of many seconds and stared up at him, wide-eyed, her lips moist and still parted, stunned by the depth of feeling he could evoke so easily.

'What the hell was Robert doing with a woman like you?' he whispered. 'I can't imagine that he knew what to do you with you.'

She pushed away from him, her eyes flashing. 'And you do, of course.'

'Oh, yes,' he drew the words out slowly. 'Yes, indeed. I know exactly what to do.' He walked away from her then, turning his head at the door. 'Cocktails in an hour,' he said perfunctorily. 'And by the the way, the Chesterfields have an old custom—we dress for dinner on Tuesday nights.'

Holly sucked in an infuriated breath. 'Well now, that's a shame, isn't it, and after all my plans to come naked!'

One side of his mouth lifted, derisively, she thought. 'I meant that we *dress* for dinner, Holly. Black tie.'

Fortunately he had turned again and was out of the door before the full colour of her embarrassment rose to her cheeks.

CHAPTER FOUR

A LITTLE defiantly, Holly pulled on a plain knit dress that was strictly afternoon wear. Black tie, indeed! What an idotic notion. She didn't know what kind of a game he was playing, but if he thought she was going to dress to the nines to sit at that big table with no one but him, he had another think coming.

The hairbrush stopped half-way between the dressing-table and her head as a thought occurred to her. What if there *were* to be other guests? What if Tuesday was traditionally a night of formal entertainment, and he had simply—no, maliciously—neglected to tell her? Something told her he was the kind of man who would enjoy seeing her make a fool of herself, just because he resented her relationship with Robert.

She closed her eyes and put the brush down carefully, shuddering to think that she might very well have walked into a room of elegantly clad strangers, dressed in a plain brown knit barely suitable for the office.

'Sorry, Daniel Chesterfield,' she told the mirror with a slightly wicked smile. 'It's not quite that easy to catch Holly Sherwood off guard.'

Half an hour later she peered into the mirror,

well satisfied with what she saw. She couldn't remember the last time she'd put this much effort into her appearance, and, even though it had been done more out of spite than an earnest desire to look attractive, the process itself had been almost fun. The woman who looked back at her would be able to hold her own in any company, no matter how elegant.

She'd bought the dress when she had started to date Robert, thinking that the number of opportunities to wear it would more than justify the exorbitant price-tag. He was a Chesterfield, after all, heir to a socially prominent family's wealth and obligations, and that meant all sorts of formal occasions.

She smiled a little wistfully, remembering how little she had known of Robert then. It was only later, after buying the dress, that she had learned how much he despised the formal advertisments of wealth, the ostentatious celebrations common to the social station to which he had been born.

'I hate these affairs,' he'd told her once, tearing up an engraved invitation to an exclusive charity ball. 'They're the worst kind of discrimination. An invitation doesn't really mean that you're invited; it means that a whole lot of other people aren't.'

And that was so typical of Robert. Humanity was the only club he belonged to, and he loved almost every member.

Holly dropped her head and pressed two fingers to the space between her brows, trying to push back the memories that kept welling up, threaten-ning to spill from her eyes.

She pulled a deep breath in through her teeth, then lifted her eyes to the mirror again. The only way she had been able to control her grief for the last year had been by suppressing all emotions entirely, and she was getting very good at it. Like now, for instance. Her face appeared lifeless, even to her, and somehow that seemed to suit her dress, her make-up and the occasion. How Robert would have hated them all!

She'd tamed the natural fullness of her hair into an intricate, obedient swirl at the nape of her neck, clipping it to immobility with a clasp of cultured pearl flowers on a delicate spray of golden stems. It looked almost painfully neat— and fake. Gone was the wide-eyed innocence of her expression, altered by artful smudges of dusky blue; and gone too was the sweet, contoured softness of her face, now carved into hardened angles through the magic of blusher. She wasn't quite sure whose face looked back at her from the mirror but, whoever it was, it certainly went with the dress. She felt a momentary twinge of regret that Robert had never seen her this way, that he had been so stubborn about avoiding any affair that required more than jeans and a shirt. The dress draped from one shoulder to the floor in a graceful cascade of midnight-blue silk, its only ornamentation the generous swells of the body beneath it, and the slender arm and rounded shoulder left bare. She knew instinctively that Daniel Chesterfield would love the way she looked almost as much as his brother would have hated it, because it was a look that belonged in his world.

'But not Robert's,' she murmured aloud, her eyes still. 'And not mine.'

Anna lifted one severe brow as Holly entered the kitchen after shedding boots and coat in the back entry. That single gesture was her sole comment on Holly's appearance. 'In the living-room.' She jerked her grey head towards the door, then turned back to the stove. 'Damn!'

A steaming bubble of fragrant sauce had exploded from the pan she was tending, spattering her hand.

Without thinking, Holly rushed over, grabbed the older woman's hand and peered down at it, frowning. 'Come on. It's starting to blister.' She literally dragged Anna over to the sink and thrust the injured hand under a gentle stream of cool water.

Her reaction had been so rapid that Anna almost forgot to protest at the familiarity from a young woman she had never met before. 'What do you think you're doing?' she finally remembered to demand, her brows nearly meeting in a scowl.

'I'm stopping the burn—stop jerking your hand away—there. Just hold it under the water for a minute.'

'You're splashing your dress.'

'It'll dry.'

'Well, my hand won't if you hold it under there much longer. Let go, for crying out loud! It's just a couple of tiny spots. See! They're hardly red. I've had worse burns than this from standing under a light bulb.'

Holly examined the hand carefully, then stepped away with a shrug. 'I guess it wasn't as bad as it looked.'

Anna's gaze was sharp, as always, but a flicker of confusion lingered in the old eyes. They burned into Holly's back as she left the kitchen.

She shook her wet hand as if to scatter the residue of Holly's touch, and went back to her work.

The living-room was a fairy-tale tapestry of pastel: a garden of pale rose and ice-green furnishings planted on a carpet of white. Holly felt shockingly out of place as she entered in the swirls of her dark gown—like a black flower in a wedding bouquet.

Daniel turned from the drink caddy when she came in, and stilled when he saw her. She stopped just inside the doorway and met his eyes.

Her heart thumped in an involuntary extra beat, for no reason that she could think of—except, perhaps, the way he looked at her.

His brows were so dark—had she noticed that before?—drawing two straight lines over the blue flash of his eyes. His hair was still damp from showering, slicked back impatiently with his fingers from the look of it, and already threatening to fall forward across one side of his forehead. Her gaze drifted downward.

Damn! He wore dinner clothes better than any man she had ever seen. Better than Robert would have, she acknowledged reluctantly, remembering the broad, heavily muscled physique that had spoken more of athletics than elegance. And then she winced inwardly, feeling intensely disloyal, because Robert had suffered under that particular comparison.

She felt Daniel's gaze touch her, followed by the instant quickening of pulse and breath. What was the matter with her? She shouldn't respond like that to this man—he was the direct opposite of everything she'd loved in his brother. She struggled desperately to call Robert's face to mind like a talisman against a curse. Bright, wonderful Robert, with a spirit as light as the colour of his hair, so happily, contagiously carefree. Joy had followed him, surrounded him, touching everyone he touched, and Holly couldn't remember a single dark moment with the man. She'd loved him. Dammit, she'd *loved* him!

But he'd never made her feel like this . . .

Daniel smiled suddenly, wickedly, she thought, as if he'd been able to read her frustration, and was pleased to be the cause of it.

Oh, hell! She released a long breath and her shoulders sagged a little. Maybe he was right. Maybe this was just physical attraction in its purest form, and love had nothing to do with it, Suddenly it seemed chidish to deny it, to pretend it didn't exist, and the moment she reached that conclusion, she felt better.

'I'd like a vodka martini,' she said calmly. 'Two, if you're going to keep looking at me like that.'

His right brow and the right side of his mouth

quirked upward. 'At the risk of losing my status as
a gentleman, I'd like to point out that you've been
looking at me in exactly the same way.'

She coloured slightly, but refused to back down
from this newfound frankness. Somehow it seemed
less dangerous than denial. 'It's just a simple
physical attraction, that's all.'

He made a small sound in his throat that might
have been an expression of amusement. 'Well!
We've made a little progress. At least you've come
to the point where you're willing to admit the
obvious, but you still don't get the point. There's
nothing simple about a physical attraction, Holly.
Haven't you learned that yet?'

She dismissed what he said with an expression of
resigned tolerance, but he never saw it. He had
already turned his attention to the bottles and
glasses on the portable drink caddy. She found a
comfortable chair while he was distracted, but had
to press her lips together against a smile when he
handed her two martins at once.

His breath caressed her forehead as he bent to
hand her the drinks. 'You said you wanted two if I
intended to keep looking at you like this. I do.'

She smiled and set one drink on a side-table,
thinking that having it out in the open like this was
really better. Just having it spoken aloud
diminished the crackling sexual tension between
them. A little. So she found him attractive? So
what? He *was* attractive. Was acknowledging that
so awful?

'You wear dinner clothes very well,' she told him

as he took a chair opposite hers.

His brows lifted slightly. 'You're getting downright straightforward. You have a few drinks before you came over?'

'Would I have to be drunk to justify paying you a compliment?'

He took a long, slow swallow from his glass, his eyes never leaving hers.

She smiled into the rim of her own glass, a little uncomfortable that the position of his chair placed him directly in her line of sight. 'Besides, just because I find you attractive doesn't mean we'll end up in bed together, no matter what you may think.'

He stared at her for a long time without saying anything. Then his lips curved upward and he blinked.

Good lord, he hadn't had to say a thing. All he'd done was blink, and somehow, with that single, simple, perfectly natural gesture, he had managed to shatter her composure. Without fully realising what she was doing, Holly downed the whole of her first martini and reached for the second.

'Ah.' He leaned forward, his arms braced on his knees, bringing his eyes to within a few feet of hers. 'I think I like it better when you're just a little bit nervous.' His voice slid across the space between them like oil snaking across a warm skillet. 'Your chest flushes when you're nervous, did you know that?' he murmured, smiling. 'The colour spreads like a sunrise, all the way up your neck to your cheeks.' Holly's eyes widened slightly and she swallowed. 'Does it go down, too, Holly? Do your breasts blush when I look at them? Like this?'

'Dinner!' Anna's voice crackled from the doorway like splitting wood, and Holly jumped in her chair, hot with embarrassment, wondering how much the old lady had heard.

'Thank God,' she murmured, and in a very unladylike gesture she tossed back the rest of her second martini.

'Perhaps you'd prefer to drink your dinner,' Anna said tartly, glaring at her.

'That's enough, Anna,' Daniel said. His voice was quiet, but his eyes were hard. 'More than enough. Miss Sherwood and I will be in when we're ready.'

Anna spun on her heel and stomped out of the room.

'My God,' Holly mumbled. 'She really, really hates me, doesn't she? But why? What have I done?'

For a moment Holly thought he was actually going to answer her question. He dropped his head to stare at the floor between his knees, his brow furrowed in thought. But then he shook his head once, rose to his feet and extended a hand. 'Think you can walk to the dining-room under your own steam after two martinis?'

Holly waggled her fingers at his foolishness. 'Of course I can walk. And talk, and chew gum, if I have to.' She got to her feet readily enough, and was surprised to find them a bit unsteady. 'On the other hand,' she said meekly, 'a gentleman's arm is always welcome.'

He tucked her hand into the crook of his elbow and patted it with a small smile. 'I'll remember that.'

'Wait a minute.' She stopped dead, suddenly remembering. 'Where is everybody?'

'Everybody?'

'The other guests.'

'What made you think there would be other guests?'

She frowned impatiently, waving in a loose gesture that was meant to indicate the way they were dressed, then dropped her arm, frustrated. For some reason it didn't seem to be working right. 'This. *This,*' she repeated, as if he were being intentionally thick-headed. 'The way we're dressed. You don't dress like this unless you're having company. A party.'

He sighed and nudged her gently into the dining-room, then into her seat. 'Oh, but I do. Every Tuesday night.'

'That's silly.'

'Most family traditions are, but be that as it may, the Chesterfields dress for dinner one night a week, guests or no guests.'

Holly made a face. 'That's a silly tradition,' she said petulantly, a little worried that he might think she'd gone to all this trouble to impress *him*. 'You can't tell me Robert went along with such nonsense.'

Daniel froze at the mention of his brother's name, as did Anna. She was half-way through the swinging door that led to the kitchen, a tray balanced in one hand, her gaze riveted on Holly, and suddenly Holly couldn't countenance her malice for one more moment.

'Oh, honestly,' she snapped, 'look at yourselves, both of you! All I did was mention his name, and you look like I just killed the family dog, or something.'

'Be quiet, Holly,' Daniel said, but he was looking at Anna, not her. His voice sounded strangely empty.

Anna stood frozen in the doorway for what seemed like a very long time. When she finally approached to serve the first course, she moved stiffly, like someone learning to walk again after a long, debilitating illness.

After she had left the room, Daniel tasted his consommé, then laid his spoon on his plate with exaggerated care and lifted his eyes. 'I told you last night that I would not discuss my brother . . .'

'You told me it would be *better* if we didn't. You didn't forbid the topic.'

'And it would be better. Surely you can see that now.'

Holly's gazed wavered downward as she tried to focus on her three bowls of soup. 'I can barely see *anything,*' she mumbled sullenly. Then she lifted her head and tried to hold it steady. 'Could it be that you didn't put enough mixer in those martinis you gave me?'

Amazingly, he cracked a smile. 'Holly, there *is* no mixer in a martini. Just straight booze.'

Her lips parted, then came together a little crookedly. 'No kidding?'

He was still smiling at her, and she decided that she liked that very much. 'Good grief, Holly. How did you get to be this old without knowing what was in a martini?'

'I'm not a bartender,' she scowled at him.

He pressed his napkin to his mouth and held it there for a moment. When he took it away, the smile was gone, and his face looked very stern indeed. 'Eat,' he directed her with a gesture, and because she would have done anything he asked at that moment she complied.

Half-way through the main course she regained enough of her senses to realise she had lost most of them earlier, and made a few feeble efforts at scintillating conversation to cover her embarrassment, but Daniel was oddly quiet and unresponsive. After the meal he walked her to the guest-house, saw her safely inside, then admonished her with the surprisingly tender touch of a forefinger to her nose. 'Right to bed, now. I'd like to get an early start on the book tomorrow.'

She stood at the door for a long time after he'd closed it behind him, wishing he hadn't left so soon, then scolding herself for wishing that at all. She lay awake in the big empty bed for nearly an hour, trying to put the pieces of Daniel Chesterfield together, wondering if she would ever really know him.

For years she had read the acidic, ruinous prose of his column, watched it topple public and private citizens alike, a little morbidly curious about the viciousness of a man who could shatter lives so blithely with the stroke of a pen. And at first glance he had been just what she had expected; he had matched his dark reputation perfectly. But the more time she spent with him, the more she thought there might be another man behind the name; a man who treated both slightly drunk dinner guests and irascible housekeepers with the same gentle patience. It was impossible to put that man together with the author of Daniel Chesterfield's scathing columns. Then again, the violence was certainly there, exploding to the surface whenever Robert's name was mentioned. He'd hated Robert. She no longer doubted that. And for some reason, so had Anna, and that just didn't make sense.

She snuggled deeper under the covers, wondering for the first time if she had known Robert as well as she'd thought. He'd seemed the gentlest man in the world; universally loved, and loving universally. But how could a man like that inspire the kind of hatred she'd seen in this house in less than two days? It was as if Daniel and Anna remembered a different man entirely—a man Holly had never met . . .

CHAPTER FIVE

AN OVERNIGHT snow had dusted the world with an inch of sparkling powder that sliced the morning sunlight into prisms and shot it back up into the air. The grounds glittered under a blinding blanket of new white that made Holly's eyes water when she looked at it. It was the first time she'd seen the back garden in the morning, and it looked as if someone had dressed it especially for the occasion.

The snow-laden boughs of the pines trembled slightly as she closed the guest-house door behind her, sending showers of white crystals to the ground beneath. She smiled and shoved unmittened hands into the pockets of her jacket, then scuffed between the shovelled banks of the path towards the main house. For a moment she felt guilty for marring the scene with the tracks of her passing, but then she noticed someone else's bootprints had already stomped across the new snow, packing it down close to the house. Probably Anna, she thought; out here crushing the sparkles underfoot because they were pretty.

She closed her eyes and pulled a last breath of the crisp air deep into her lungs before entering the house, saddened by the prospect of spending such a glorious day indoors.

Daniel swung open the back door just as she reached for the knob, almost as if he'd been standing there waiting for her. She caught her breath in surprise.

'You startled me.'

'Did I?' It wasn't a question; just one of those meaningless phrases people say to assure you that they're paying attention.

She shifted her weight nervously from one foot to the other as he stood there staring down at her, blocking the doorway. He wore a blousy, long-sleeved white shirt, loosely tucked into dark trousers, and he looked more like a pirate then ever.

'Where's your hat?' he demanded, dark brows lowered.

'My hat?' She put a bare hand to her head.

'Yes, your hat. You're not wearing one. You lose over half of your body heat through your head, and it's barely zero out there. Get inside before you freeze to death.' He grabbed her by the elbow and pulled her through the doorway. 'Good lord! No mittens, either?'

There was no gentle concern in either his words or his expression, but the chastisement sounded so much like what a parent might say to an errant child that it made her laugh.

'Oh, good grief.' She chafed her hands together. 'It's only a few yards from the guest-house, and I hate hats. Mittens, too. I hardly ever wear them. Besides, it doesn't feel very cold. It's just beautiful out there, isn't it?'

Her grin faded under his unrelenting scowl. To avoid looking at it, she busied herself hanging up her jacket and stomping the snow off her tennis shoes on to the mat. When she looked up again he was standing with his hands on his hips, staring at her wet feet.

'I know, I know.' She flapped her arms in exasperation. 'No boots, either, but I'm too old to scold, so give it up.'

His eyes flicked up and down her body in a cursory, seemingly apathetic inspection. 'Looks like you wore everything you own today. The house *is* heated, you know.'

Holly glanced down briefly, a little embarrassed. She hadn't even thought about the clothes she'd pulled on so hastily back in the guest-house—heavy brown corduroy slacks, a white turtleneck, and over that a brown flannel shirt that hung open nearly to her knees. It was the kind of outfit one would wear to cross-country ski, or hike through the woods—too many warm clothes for a day inside by a fireplace. She wondered if subconsciously she'd been trying to put as many barriers between Daniel Chesterfield and herself as possible.

He teased her with a smile. 'I liked the housecoat better.'

She pushed past him, blushing furiously, into the empty kitchen. 'Where's Anna?'

She turned in a small circle as she looked around, half expecting the ill-tempered housekeeper to pop out from behind a cupboard and snarl at her.

'It's Anna's day off. She won't be back until tonight.'

'Really?' She looked like a kid who'd just learned all the schools were closed, and Daniel could barely contain a smile.

He nodded towards a coffee-maker on the far counter. 'Mugs are in the overhead cupboard. Help yourself. Did you have breakfast before you came over?'

She nodded as she poured coffee in a mug for herself, and then in the one he held out for a refill. It was the first time she'd seen his hands this close, and the weight of the coffee-pot was suddenly unbearably heavy. He has beautiful hands, she thought, admiring the long, straight fingers that cupped the mug in a relaxed curve; but then she remembered that those hands had been beneath her robe only yesterday. Her own hand trembled and she had to concentrate to pour the scalding liquid into the cup, and not over his fingers.

She saw the mug lift slightly in a gesture of silent thanks, but was afraid to look directly up into his eyes. 'Well, shall we go directly to the library?' she spoke at the floor.

'Not yet. I usually have my coffee out here.'

She followed him over to the windowside table, then stopped, staring out at where the grounds rolled away under the snow to a distant bank of iced pines. 'Oh, this is lovely,' she murmured, lips parted in appreciation.

'You should eat here all the time, instead of in that huge, empty dining-room.'

'I do, most of the time.' He slid into the chair next to hers and propped his forearms on the table, very close to her own. His gaze was fixed on a point just outside the window. 'Look at that,' he murmured. 'I put out a full measure of seeds less than an hour ago, and already the bluejays have eaten most of it.'

Holly let her eyes follow his to the birdfeeder, its pole half buried in snow, standing a few yards from the house. 'Oh,' she said almost to herself, smiling at the colourful flurry of wings as several bluejays bickered for position. 'Those were your tracks outside, then. I thought maybe Anna had been out there, stamping all the sparkles out of the snow.'

For once, he hadn't been able to stop the laugh. It burst from his throat with the staccato of spontaneity, and Holly turned her head slowly to look at him; 'My God! You have a sense of humour.'

He turned back to the window and shook his head, as if the laugh had been a lapse that wouldn't happen again, but the trace of a smile lingered on his lips. 'I like to start every day right here, when I can,' he said thoughtfully. 'That's the real world out there.' He nodded at the birdfeeder, now stage to a multitude of feathered players.

It seemed like a capricious comment at first, but the longer Holly watched the frantic scramble at the feeder, the more appropriate it became. Three days ago she'd been panicked about finding a place to live during her brownstone's renovation; two days before that she'd been frustrated for a full afternoon over an ad layout that just wasn't working. How insignificant those things seemed now, as she watched the fragile creatures outside struggle just to survive the barren, bitter cold of winter. In a way it was like watching a microcosm of the human condition—there was tragedy out there, and triumph, hostile prejudice between species, beauty and plainness, but above it all a sense of immutable order; a sense of things being exactly as they were supposed to be.

Somewhere in the middle of her second cup of coffee, she stopped watching the birds and started watching Daniel, thinking that she was further from understanding him than ever. How was it possible for one man to cherish the lessons of wildlife, and yet nurture a hatred so strong that it survived even the object's death?

'We stare at each other a lot, have you noticed that?'

She started slightly as she realised that he had been studying her just as she had been studying him. 'I was trying to see the resemblance between you and Robert,' she lied, so anxious to dismiss her fascination with his face that she said absolutely the wrong thing.

'There is none,' he said sharply, turning his head away so forcefully that it lifted the curtain of black from his forehead. 'We were as different as it's possible for brothers to be.'

Even as she thought how true that statement was, she tried to deny it. 'You had to share an odd gene or two—you had to be alike in some ways.'

'No!' There was a desperate quality to the anger in his voice, a warning in the eyes that darkened instantly to that alarming shade of navy blue.

'But he was your brother . . .'

'I don't need reminding of that!'

' . . . how in God's name could you have hated him?'

She felt the crushing weight of his disdain as his eyes shifted slowly to meet hers. 'And how in God's name could you have loved him?'

Holly hesitated for a moment, and then whispered helplessly, 'It was impossible not to. Everybody loved Robert.'

One side of his mouth lifted in what seemed like slow motion, and Holly felt herself tense, as if anticipating a blow.

He continued to stare at her, searching for something in her face, and then finally he dropped his eyes, stood up slowly, tiredly, and left the table to cross the room towards the door. 'Come on. there's more coffee in the library. It's time we got to work.'

It took Holly a few moments before she could bring herself to follow him, and when she did she kept her eyes cast down, counting the large tiles on the hall as they walked the length of the house.

Thirty-three. She finished her silent count as she turned and paused at the top of the shallow steps, facing the mantel painting that smiled at her from across the library. Unconsciously, forgetting for a moment the quarrel in the kitchen, she smiled back at the picture, as if it were alive. It seemed so real that she had to catch herself before greeting the woman aloud.

'That's your mother, isn't it?' she asked softly.

Daniel stopped half-way across the room and looked over at the painting. 'Yes.'

'She was beautiful.'

'Yes. She was.'

Holly glanced at him, understanding from his tone that this was yet another subject they would not talk about. When she'd asked Robert about his parents, all he'd been able to choke out was that they were both dead, and that he couldn't talk about them. It was too painful. Apparently this was true for Daniel as well.

But I wonder what she was like, she mused, staring up at the woman who seemed to be looking pointedly at her, trying to tell her something.

'Her name was Rebecca,' Daniel said quietly. 'You would have liked her.'

Holly smiled wistfully. Yes, I would have liked you, Rebecca. I can see that. I wish I had had the chance.

The hours passed quickly as they sorted through hundreds of photographs Daniel had collected through the years: vignettes of countless mothers and children, the silent expression of their relationships trapped for ever in glossy prints. Holly became immersed in her task, fighting the emotional tug of each picture, concentrating only on separating them into stacks according to the mood they evoked: nostalgia, empathy, sorrow, heartbreak . . . Each face told a story, and each story was so emotionally moving that Holly found herself fighting tears more often than not, swallowing frequently to relieve the tightness of her throat. Whatever else he was, Daniel was a genius with a camera, particularly in capturing the essence of human feeling. It seemed almost criminal that his gift had remained undiscovered; and yet there was something missing in the collection of photographs, something she couldn't pinpoint. As she worked, she imagined all the photographs arranged in a book, and although the book would be magnificent, envisaging it left an empty space in her heart that she continued to puzzle over.

'You don't think we should divide the book into section by country, or parts of the world?' he asked her at one point.

Holly didn't even look up. She just smiled and shook her head. 'Motherhood doesn't have a nationality,' she murmured in reply, still distracted by the elusive missing factor. 'The relationship between mother and child is the same everywhere. It would be wrong to let boundaries or politics divide one of the few things that brings all of the people in the world together. This is what we all have in common.'

Daniel's eyes stilled and focused on her face, but she was so preoccupied that she didn't notice, any more than she had noticed that he had done very little since they had started. He just stood on the

opposite side of the long table where she worked,
watching her face more than what she was doing
with her hands. In a matter of moments she had
taken over the project, making it hers as well as his.
He supplied the raw material, she refined it,
aligned it, envisaging the final product that would
say what he had wanted to say in the first place, but
couldn't express.

'You're very good,' he told her. 'Better than I
thought. Perhaps better than even you know.'

She lifted her head and smiled at him, and he
smiled back. For the first time since they had met,
they exchanged a moment uncluttered by the ghost
of Robert that haunted them both.

'It's not me.' She dropped her eyes modestly,
gesturing at the pictures. 'They arrange themselves.
They're exquisite, all of them. What I don't
understand is why the book wasn't finished long
ago.'

Daniel sighed, pushed the fingers of one hand
back through his hair, then walked over to the
fireplace and stood looking up at the painting of
his mother, his back to her. 'Robert and I couldn't
agree on the concept. We fought over every
picture. Had he lived, I doubt that this book would
ever have been published.'

Holly opened her mouth to ask why, then
thought better of pursuing any subject that
involved Robert. Instead, she reached for the last
box of photographs and pulled it towards her. 'Are
these anything special? The box is taped shut.'

He looked over his shoulder briefly. 'They're

throwaways.'

'Throwaways?' She smiled and started to peel away the tape. 'From what I've seen, you're incapable of taking a throwaway picture.'

She pulled the top photo out and felt her heart constrict, and then soar. It was the missing factor, the warm, glorious filler for the empty space she'd felt. Suddenly it came together, and this time her vision for the book was complete. 'Oh, Daniel,' she murmured, so intent on the photograph that she didn't notice the blackness of his expression as he spun to face her.

Lord, how had he captured such a moment? Every picture she had seen so far was a testament to the love between mother and child transcending the bleak realities of poverty and suffering. There had been photos of the malnourished from third world nations; photos of farming mothers and migrant workers struggling in the fields that fed others; and the startling, empty faces of desperate, inner-city mothers and children who just barely clung to the joy of love over the trials of life. All of the photographs had glorified the triumph of a mother's love over the worst kinds of adversity. But this one . . . this one was different.

The toddler was a fair-haired, roly-poly replica of her pretty young mother. She had one chubby arm extended, an absurd, battered daisy clutched in a tiny fat fist. Daniel had clicked the shutter just as the mother reached for her child's first gift, and the two faces were alight with the joy of giving, and the joy of receiving. There were no shadows in the sunlit photo—neither real, nor implied. No spectre of poverty or suffering to spoil the purity of the moment, and it was breathtakingly beautiful. This photograph would be the cover of the book, she decided instantly. It had to be.

Daniel stomped over to the table from the fire place, snatched the picture from her, glanced at it, then tossed it aside, face down. 'It says nothing. It's ordinary. Every kid picks a flower for his mother at one time in his life. There's nothing special about it.'

Holly frowned at him. 'But that's exactly why it is special, Daniel,' she said softly. 'To all of us. Because we've all lived that moment, and at the time it was magic. Somehow you captured that feeling and saved it, so that everyone who looks at it can remember.'

His face hardened. 'They're happy.' He flipped the photograph right side up and jabbed at it with one accusatory finger. 'Look at them. They're *happy*.'

'Of course they're happy.' Her voice was barely above a whisper. 'That's the biggest part of motherhood, isn't it? The joy . . .'

His voice exploded as he leaned across the table towards her, quivering forearms braced on white-knuckled fists. 'No wonder you and Robert got along so well! You were a perfectly matched set, weren't you? Two smiling fools, closing your eyes to everything unpleasant, everything ugly, everything painful! God forbid you should ever have to see the world as it really is! Neither one of you had the guts to look at it! I should have known you'd agree with him!'

Holly took a slow step backwards, away from the table, her eyes wide and fixed. 'What do you mean, agree with him?'

His arm flung sideways at the box she'd just opened. 'Those! Those insipid, smiling, happy-ever-after pictures! *They* were the book Robert wanted! *That* was the portrait of his idea of motherhood!'

Holly stood motionless, a little numbed by the outburst, and by the sudden flash of under-standing. 'I see,' she murmured. 'Robert wanted to use these, and only these. The happy pictures. And you wanted to use only the others.'

Daniel scowled at her statement of the obvious.

'You were both wrong,' she said quietly, but steadily. Daniel's eyes shot dark blue sparks that made her flinch and catch her breath, but she went on, 'Or maybe you were both right. The relation-ship between mother and child isn't all sweetness and light and joy.' She smiled tentatively, thinking that indeed that was the way Robert would have wanted it to be. Daniel was right about that much. His brother never could bear to see suffering of any kind. 'But it isn't all struggle and pain, either. It's all of those things put together. It's part of your vision, and it's part of Robert's, too. Can't you see that?'

He still leaned on the table, and it rocked slightly under the pressure of his hands. His face was drawn and colourless, making his eyes stand out like chips of dark fire. 'You'll never stop defending his cowardice, will you?'

'I'm not defending Robert!' she shouted. The echo of her voice hung in the room, then gradually faded as other sounds trickled into Holly's consciousness—the muted crackle of the fire, the faint hum of a massive furnace somewhere beneath them, the soft, slightly irregular sound of Daniel's breath as if was forced through his lips.

She was afraid to take her eyes from his, although she wasn't quite sure why. What did she think he would do? Leap over the table and attack her the moment she relaxed her guard? Still, she kept watching him.

The table-top creaked when he finally pushed himself back and straightened to his full height. Unexpectedly, he was the one who broke eye contact and looked around absently, as if he'd forgotten where he was and what he was doing there.

'That's enough work for now,' he said tonelessly, walking towards the door. 'Do what you like with the rest of the day.'

Holly stared after him helplessly, wanting to call him back, but then wondering what she would say if she did. She caught herself wishing desperately that they could recapture that single moment when their interaction had not been cluttered with Robert's memory, when it had finally seemed that they were truly alone. They had been in sync then, for the briefest space of time, two people in tune with each other, appreciating each other.

But Robert hadn't been a part of that moment, and she suddenly felt guilty for enjoying anything that excluded him. After all, the most precious of her memories revolved around Robert, and the time they had had together. How callous to be willing to sacrifice them, just to make life with his brother and this job a little easier.

She sighed and glanced down at the table. The picture Daniel had flipped over with such contempt had landed, ironically, on the photo of a mother bent over the wasted form of her dying child. One shot was joy, one was pathos; but love was in both. Opposite sides of the same coin. Just like Robert and Daniel. The picture had to come together to make the story complete, and perhaps the brothers did, too.

CHAPTER SIX

IT JUST wasn't working. Nothing was working. Not the book, not trying to communicate with Daniel, not even this damn omelette.

Holly looked down at the mess of eggs and vegetables sticking to the pan, threw the spatula down in disgust and shoved the skillet off the burner.

'I can't even cook any more,' she grumbled aloud, stomping into the cosy living-room and plopping down on the couch that faced the fire. She glared at the cheery flames as if they were to blame for her ruined supper, and then at the unread book lying face down on the coffee-table. With one vicious swipe, she knocked it to the floor, then crossed her arms over her chest and just sat there, scowling.

It was Monday of her second week at the Chesterfield estate. Daniel had disappeared to wherever it was he disappeared to on Mondays, taking Anna with him, and Holly was alone with the decidedly unpleasant memories of a week gone bad.

Work on the book was at a standstill. For the sake of what she believed had the potential to be an outstanding work of art, Holly continued to push for inclusion of some of the photos Robert had chosen. To her frustration, every time she'd broached the subject, Daniel had exploded and stomped from the room in a rage.

'You're impossible!' she'd shrieked at him yesterday morning 'You're going to ruin what could be a great book, just to spite a man who's been dead for a year! What's the matter? Didn't you have the guts to fight it out with Robert when he was still alive?'

Even now, a full day later, she couldn't believe she'd said that. She shuddered, remembering the way Daniel had glared at her before leaving the room. She hadn't seen him since, but had spent every one of the last twenty-four hours waiting to be dismissed, waiting for Anna to come trotting out to the guest-house with a maliciously smug smile to tell her to pack up and get out. It hadn't happened yet, but that didn't mean it wouldn't.

She leaned her head back on the couch and closed her eyes, wondering how she would take it when the moment finally came; not so much how she would react, but how she would *feel* when she lost this job and was forced to leave. The prospect left her tense but, oddly enough, not panicked. If the worst came to the worst, she could have her old job at the paper back, and Hampton and Jeanine would surely take her in until her brownstone was finished. Practically speaking, life would go on, and she would survive. But perhaps survival wasn't enough any more.

For one thing, she had fallen in love with the

book, with what the book could be, if Daniel
would only let it happen. She wanted desperately to
be a part of its creation, to guide it to its full
potential. Leaving that to another, or worse yet,
leaving it undone, was unthinkable.

And there was something more . . . something
compelling about living here. Maybe it was just
because it had been Robert's home, and she still
clung tenaciously to his memory, reluctant to leave
the grounds where he had walked, the people he had
known. And yet the compulsion to stay was a dark
one, a fearful one, because the people here had hated
him, and she wasn't sure she wanted to know why.

At first she'd wondered why Daniel hadn't
explained his hatred of Robert—she would have
thought he'd jump at the chance to slander his
dead brother, his hate was so strong. But then
she'd decided that the reason had to be petty,
something silly and insubstantial, like simple
sibling jealousy. He would never admit to
something like that, and had it been more, if
Robert had really done something despicable,
something deserving of such hatred, Daniel would
have wanted her to know, right? He'd love the
satisfaction of destroying Robert's memory in the
eyes of the woman who'd loved him.

And there was one last reason she didn't want to
be fired—a reason she didn't care to examine too
closely. The simple truth was that she didn't want
to think about not seeing Daniel every day. In a
perverse sort of way she seemed to feed on his
black moods and volatile temper, as if she needed

a daily confrontation to satisfy some bizarre addiction for combat. And yet it wasn't like her to be attracted to conflict. That certainly wasn't what had attracted her to Robert. His kindness, his generosity, his trusting nature—those were the things she had loved about him, and they all found their exact opposite in Daniel. So why was she drawn to him?

She kept telling herself that it wasn't Daniel that pulled at her, that she was only hoping to discover in him some remnant of his brother, but the rationalisation was wearing thin. It was Daniel's eyes she felt touching her, making her feel alive again; Daniel's voice she waited to hear; Daniel's face that hovered in her dreams—not Robert's.

She sighed, lifting her heavy hair from her neck, tipping her head forward to stare into the fire. It crackled in an echo of the same tension that had been with her since she'd moved in, and for a moment she longed for the peace of the times she'd spent with Robert. The baggy shirt she was wearing shifted on the bare breast beneath, reminding her instantly of what Daniel's hand had felt like there, and any wish for peace was banished instantly. She didn't want to feel at peace any more. She wanted to feel something else.

She turned at the click of the latch and the icy blast of wind from the doorway.

'Hello.' Daniel sagged against the door, closing it. His hair was tousled and wet, and new snow sprinkled the shoulders of his dark sweater. He hoisted a dusty bottle of wine in one gloveless, hand, reddened by the cold. 'It's a peace offering. The best Beaujolais in the cellar. I thought if we both got drunk enough, we might be able to talk without screaming at each other.'

Holly blinked at him over the arm she had flung across the back of the couch, then nodded once at the bottle. 'That probably isn't enough to keep the peace.'

He pulled another bottle from beneath his sweater and held it up in his other hand, and she laughed.

'You're soaking wet, and you look frozen. Where did you leave your coat?'

He made his way to the fireplace and turned his back to the flames, looking down at her. 'The same place you always leave your mittens and hat.' He set both bottles on the coffee-table and pulled a corkscrew from the front pocket of a pair of faded jeans. 'Well? How about it? Are you going to get some glasses, or are you going to kick me out?'

'I thought I was the one who was going to get kicked out.'

He shrugged impatiently. 'What for? Talking back to the boss?'

'Something like that.'

'Hell, Anna's been doing that for years, and she still here.'

'I get the feeling Anna's a special case.'

He looked right at her. 'So are you.'

For no other reason than to escape his eyes, she got up and went to the kitchen. 'I thought you were gone on Mondays,' she called over her shoulder.

'I never go so far that I can't be back for supper. It's about that time, you know. Have you eaten?'

'Not yet.'

'Good. We'll both have this on an empty stomach, then. Shouldn't drink it any other way.'

By the time she returned with two tulip glasses, he had both bottles open and breathing, and was slouched happily in the armchair that sat at a right angle to the couch; the same armchair Holly had sat in the afternoon his hands had found their way under her robe.

He filled both glasses nearly to the rim, then lifted his in a toast. 'One entire glass,' he said firmly. 'That's the deal. We each drink one glass of wine before we say a word to each other.'

Holly smiled, nodded her agreement, and tucked her legs under her before taking her first sip.

It was a good wine, too good to be hurried; and, strangely enough, so was sitting here with Daniel Chesterfield without exchanging a single word. It wasn't the way she would have planned it. She would have dressed differently, had she known he was coming—in her rose lounging robe perhaps, with her hair up and her eyes shadowed and her lips glossed. But maybe it was better that she hadn't had time to prepare, to anticipate, to get nervous. As it was now, sitting here in old jeans and a baggy shirt, with loose hair and freshly scrubbed face, she was reasonably comfortable, like someone who had received an unexpected visit from a friend.

The wine slid down smoothly, the fire crackled a merry accompaniment, and the windows grew dark as they drank.

'Don't do that.' He reached over and caught her wrist as she reached for the lamp switch.

She eased her hand down slowly from the lamp, her eyes searching the shadows of his face. He held on to her wrist a little longer than necessary.

'I can't see your eyes with the fire behind you like that.'

He hesitated for a moment, then moved from the armchair to sit next to her on the couch. She turned sideways to face him and saw the golden reflections of the fire dancing in his eyes. 'Better?'

No, she thought, it's not better; but she forced a small smile and nodded.

'Robert is ruining the book,' he said steadily.

Suddenly the peace of the moment was shattered. With the mention of Robert's name came the presence of Robert, hovering in the shadows, reminding her that this was his brother, somehow chastising her for finding pleasure in his company. The weight of memory left her feeling disloyal and flat, as if all the breath had been crushed out of her.

'I'd rather not talk about Robert now,' she said quietly.

'We have to. He's interfering with our work.'

'He *can't*!' The words were wrenched from her. 'He's gone. You can't possibly blame him for things that happen a year after . . .' The sentence trailed away as she let her chin fall to her chest.

She looked up after a long silence to find Daniel staring at the fire. His features were rigid with the effort of containing his frustration.

'That's the worst part,' he said bitterly. 'That he can reach out from the grave to ruin things, just as effectively as he did when he was alive.'

'No!' The firelit swirl of her hair followed her head as she spun it to face him. 'It isn't Robert who's ruining this book, it's you! Your hatred of him! It colours everything! You can't see past it to what might be good for the book—if Robert liked it, it's wrong, as far as you're concerned, just because Robert liked it!' Her face sagged suddenly as the full realisation of her own words hit her. 'My God! You probably feel that way about me, too, don't you?' she whispered, her expression stricken. 'You resent me, just because Robert loved me . . .'

He closed his eyes briefly, and the single word 'no' escaped his lips in a whisper. 'No,' he said more strongly, looking away from her. 'If I resent you at all, it's because you loved Robert, not the other way around.'

'Oh, Daniel.' She leaned towards him, catching herself just as she was about to place a hand on his arm, pulling back at the last moment. 'Don't you see?' she begged him. 'Robert isn't ruining what we're trying to do together, but your hatred of him is. It's the only thing that survived his death.'

His eyes narrowed dangerously as she spoke, and she could barely see the glint of deep blue between the thickly fringed lids. 'That's not quite true.' He barely moved his lips as he spoke, and he never took his eyes from hers. 'What you felt for him survived his death, too, and that's where our problems lie.'

Holly inched further into the corner of the couch, retreating from the pain she heard in his voice. 'Maybe . . . maybe if I knew why you hated him so . . .'

'And maybe if I knew why you loved him . . .'

Holly felt a trembling deep in her stomach, and unconsciously wiped the hand that wasn't holding her glass against the rough fabric of the couch arm.

What if he told her something perfectly awful about Robert? What if there had been another side of the man she'd loved so totally? A dark, secretive side that would make her hate him, too? Then the beautiful memories would be gone, Robert would be gone—truly dead at last—and everything wonderful he had taught her would be diminished, soiled somehow, and something inside her would die with him.

'Let's just forget it,' she said quickly, her eyes jerking towards the fire. 'We don't have to talk about Robert. We'll just declare a truce, try it again, concentrate only on the book . . .'

'Holly.' Daniel reached over slowly, captured her chin, and turned her face towards him. She had no idea what her face looked like at that moment, but she saw him frown, saw a flash of sympathetic concern in his eyes as he looked at her, and knew that whatever he saw made him feel sorry for her.

'Don't . . .' She turned her face away and blinked rapidly, but his hand was on her chin again, turning it back towards him, towards those incredible eyes that hid more than they revealed;

eyes that made her want to cry, to run away from whatever they promised; eyes that made her forget everything except what she imagined she saw in their depths.

'Oh, dammit,' he murmured, taking her head in both hands, rocking it gently back and forth, then holding it still as he bent forward to press his lips gently against hers.

His mouth was warm and dry and tangy with wine, and Holly jerked away instantly, startled by the flash of heat that seemed to ignite at the point of contact, and radiate outwards. She had time to catch one sharp breath between parted lips before he pulled her head back to him, his fingers twisted into the loose mass of her hair.

'Daniel . . .' she protested weakly, moving her hands to press him away, then trembling as she felt the heavy, rapid beat of his heart beneath his sweater. He was leaning over her now, threatening her with his weight and his strength. He nipped gently at her lips, catching them between his, and, without intending to, she gasped at the startlingly smooth touch of his tongue.

She felt his breath break against her face in ragged, forceful exhalations that made her close her eyes, and realised too late that their hearts were pumping to the same frantic beat; that her erratic breathing echoed his; that they trembled in unison to the fevered gasps that exploded softly from their mouths when they separated. The reasons for resisting dissolved one by one in the liquid fire that coursed up from her stomach to swell in her

breasts, and just when she had finally reached the
point where there was no strength in her hands to
keep his chest pushed away, and no will in her
mind to demand it, he flung himself away from her
and collapsed against the back of the couch, his
eyes closed, his chest heaving with the force of his
breath.

'Now,' he whispered hoarsely. 'Now tell me why
you loved Robert.'

She stilled instantly, her breasts lifting the thin
fabric of her shirt with the intake of her last breath,
her eyes wide with a kind of horrified shock. Was
that what this was all about? A preliminary to sully
the memory of Robert? To mock what she had felt
for him, to draw some sort of sick comparison
between the impulsive, purely physical desire she
had just exhibited, and the spirituality of the love
Robert had given her? Did Daniel really think the
two could be compared at all?

Her eyelids lowered slightly, shading a sudden
flatness that hardened her brown eyes. She
straightened her shirt, sat erect on the couch, and
reached for her glass without once looking at him.
'No,' she said firmly. 'This isn't the time.'

'Why?' he said scornfully. 'Because you can't
relate your feelings for Robert to what you're
feeling now?' So quickly that she had no time to
think to stop him, he pressed one hand beneath her
left breast. His smile was smug as he felt the erratic
flutter of her heart, and knew that he was the
cause. 'Because Robert never made you feel this?'

'Stop it!' She slapped his hand away and leaped

from the couch, breathing hard. Her fists were clenched at her sides as she glared down at him. 'Get out. I don't want you here.'

He linked his fingers behind his head, his eyes half closed, his smile insolent. 'Yes, you do. And just to prove to you how much, I'm going to leave.'

He rose from the couch and stood in front of her, and suddenly he seemed much taller than he had ever been before. Her neck creaked as she tipped it back to look up at him, and her eyes seemed to dry out instantly from the force of her glare.

There was a frightening smugness to his smile that made her want to back away, but she refused to be intimidated. In the next instant she wished she had, and pride be damned, for he grabbed the back of her neck and kissed her hard, and she almost cried because her body betrayed her will, leaning into him, trembling as his lips softened and worked hers.

She gasped when he released her, and kept her eyes closed so she wouldn't have to look at his satisfaction at proving his point, and his power.

She opened her eyes when she felt the rush of cold air from the door, and watched him walk out into the snowy night.

Damn you, she thought bitterly, her nails digging into the flesh of her palms. Damn you for being able to walk away.

CHAPTER SEVEN

HOLLY had expected to spend Tuesdays alone. It was the day Daniel wrote his weekly column, and initially she'd looked forward to the freedom of unscheduled time, the indulgence of reading for hours on end, or simply listening to her thoughts tick away the moments. But there was no pleasure between the covers of a book today, and the last thing she wanted to do was listen to her own thoughts. There was too much of Daniel in them.

By late afternoon she was pacing the confines of the guest-house like a caged animal, mentally kicking herself for not arranging a day in the city. That was what she should have done, of course; it was just what she needed. A day away from the pervading tension of the Chesterfield estate; a day in the bustle of one of the world's great cities preparing for Christmas. Maybe it wasn't too late. Maybe she could call Hampton and Jeanine, arrange to meet them for supper and a show . . .

She jumped when the phone rang under her hand, and snatched it from its cradle with a jerk. 'Hello!' she nearly shouted into the receiver.

'Holly? Is anything wrong?'

She closed her eyes at the sound of his voice and pressed one hand to her midsection. It couldn't possibly get any worse than this, could it? When just hearing him speak made her heart race and her blood surge so forcefully that already her face felt hot . . .

'Holly? Are you there?'

'Yes!' She stopped for a deep breath and brought her voice under control. In the silence she heard him hum softly, as if he'd begun to chuckle, then thought better of it.

'Put on some warm clothes,' he said. 'You and I need to get away from this place. I'll meet you in the driveway in twenty minutes.'

He hung up without waiting for a response, and her mouth dropped open at his impudence. Did he think she would jump at his command? Drop everything and go wherever he wanted to take her at a moment's notice?

For a moment she considered letting him sit out there alone until spring came—but only for a moment. Then she was flying into the bedroom, tearing at drawers, selecting one outfit after another casting the rejects on to the growing heap at her feet. She didn't know if it was the diversion that excited her, or the prospect of an evening away from this place with Daniel, and she didn't stop to ponder the question. she wasn't sure she wanted to know the answer.

Warm clothes, he had said, and that was fine with her. The more clothes between her body and any accidental contact with his, the better off she'd be.

She settled on a long, camel skirt that brushed

the ankes of her boots and matched her cape, then
topped it with a bulky, sexless sweater that
effectively concealed any evidence of her
femininity. Even with her cape off, he'd have to be
a very desperate man indeed to find anything erotic
in such shapelessness.

Convinced that she was totally undesirable from
the neck down, she felt perfectly safe in
accentuating a little of what she had from the neck
up. She warmed her face with bronze blush and
deep slashes of taupe eyeshadow, then brushed her
hair until it crackled with electricity. It curled over
her shoulders in an opaque curtain that seemed to
have a life of its own, but to Holly it just looked
unmanageable.

'I'm ready,' she whispered at the mirror a full
fifteen minutes after her first headlong rush into
the bedroom; and then she realised her mistake.
Looking into mirrors was a very dangerous thing
after last night. She had learned that this morning,
peering into the bathroom mirror with bleary eyes.
But she hadn't seen the bleary eyes, or the faint
shadows beneath from lack of sleep. As a matter of
fact, she hadn't even seen her own reflection.

For some reason, her gaze had focused on her
mouth, but it hadn't seemed like her mouth at all.
She felt dissociated from the woman in the mirror,
as if they had no connection whatsoever. She was
Holly Sherwood, standing in nightgown and bare
feet, mesmerised by the reflection of a mouth that
had felt the strident, sometimes cruel pressure of
Daniel Chesterfield's lips just a few short hours

before. She'd stared at her lips, not recognising them at all, stunned by the force of the memory they evoked. She could almost feel his mouth on hers, the pressure of his fingers digging into the back of her neck, and finally she had had to brace herself against the sink to remain upright.

She felt the same response as she glanced into the mirror now, felt the same throbbing in the pit of her stomach as she looked at the woman she thought of in only one way—a woman who had been handled by Daniel.

She turned away quickly and headed for the door, hoping that the frigid December air would cool the fiery flush on her cheeks, or at least give her an excuse for it.

It was only when she rounded the front of the house and approached the drive that she realised she had never seen Daniel in a car before. If she'd thought about it, she would have pictured him in precisely the kind of car he was waiting in now—a long, sleek melding of polished chrome and glistening black, with carriage lights and plush seats and enough digital controls on the dashboard to justify a co-pilot. It spoke of luxury and comfort, and in that context it seemed to suit her image of Daniel. Robert would have hated it, decrying it as tasteless ostentation in a world where so many were hungry.

Daniel jumped out to open the passenger door for her, a dark, vampish figure in the swirls of a black topcoat. It was too cold for even abbreviated greetings out in the night air, and neither said anything until they were both inside the car.

He watched her as she settled herself in the seat. 'Ready?'

Only after she had nodded did he engage the gears.

She watched the banked snow of the drive roll slowly by her window, as if the scenery were moving and they were standing still. Her right hand strayed to an array of silver buttons that would adjust her seat to any of fifty-seven positions. 'The car suits you,' she murmured.

'Well, that's odd.' His eyes searched the driveway's surface, watching for ice. 'This was Robert's car. Mine is a little sports model. Fun but cramped. I thought you might be more comfortable in this.'

'But . . . Robert drove a little economy car . . . grey, with bad shocks and great mileage and . . .'

'He only drove that to work.'

Holly frowned as she rubbed her hand on the velvety upholstery, trying to imagine unpretentious Robert in this vehicle.

'He actually . . . drove this?'

Daniel nodded absently as he turned out on to the picturesque lane. 'Of course he did. He loved this car.' He glanced at her quickly, scowled, then shook his head in disgust. 'God, you didn't know a thing about him, did you?' He laughed bitterly. 'No wonder you're surprised. This car doesn't exactly fit the altruistic image Robert painted of himself, does it?'

'It's . . . it's just a car,' she insisted, wishing she

didn't feel the need to defend Robert.

'Stupid,' Daniel was shaking his head, muttering to himself. 'Stupid of me to drive this thing, tonight of all nights. It's just like taking Robert along, when what I really wanted was for us to leave him behind.'

Holly looked straight ahead for a moment, lips pressed tightly together. The evening was turning into a disaster before it had even begun, all because Robert's name had crept into the conversation again. Either she changed the mood right now, or they might as well turn around and go back to the house.

She took a deep breath and turned sideways in the seat to face him, flinging one arm across the back in a planned, seemingly casual gesture.

'So,' she forced lightness into her tone, 'where are we going?'

He shrugged as if it didn't matter, his face sullen. 'To a restaurant right on the harbour.'

'Would I know it?'

'Not unless you patronise places with cracked crockery and wooden floors and occasional brawls.'

'Sounds irresistible.'

His mouth twitched a little, and he seemed to relax. 'Actually, it is. Great seafood, great beer, and nice people.'

'You like seafood?'

He actually smiled. 'I'd trade my soul for the right lobster.'

'So that's what happened to it.'

His smile broadened and the tension in the car seemed to dissipate, making it all right to lean back and breathe normally again. If she were very, very careful not to say anything that would make him think of Robert, perhaps they could have a cease-fire for the evening, if not a peace.

After the almost hypnotic lull of the main road, Holly was jolted to attention as they turned off on to a broken tarmac road that paralleled the harbour, and then on to a dark side street with looming frame buildings and the dank look of a place that is perpetually wet. She caught a glimpse of a hulking man in a seaman's cap darting into an alley, and fought the urge to push the automatic door-lock button.

Daniel pulled the car to the kerb in front of wooden building with a crooked front porch and two bare bulbs in wire cages flanking a door, and Holly almost groaned aloud. Surely this couldn't be the place?

'It's better inside.' He smiled at her doubtful expression. 'Really.'

He helped her out of her coat in a narrow entry-way that boasted a row of hooks on the wall, and nothing else. His brows lifted at her baggy sweater. 'My Great-Aunt Hilda had a sweater like that,' he said with a straight face. 'Broke every scale she ever stood on, that woman.'

'It's warm,' Holly said indignantly.

He chuckled with his mouth closed. 'The hell it is. It's armour.'

She pressed her lips into a straight line and

decided not to argue the point.

If she had dressed defensively, he had done the opposite, although she was quite sure that his choice had been careless, with none of the agonising that had gone into hers. He wore a body-hugging cashmere sweater of the palest blue, with a V-neck that drew her eyes to the linear definition of his chest muscles beneath the thin fabric. Cashmere had always tempted her. She clasped her hands behind her back to keep from reaching out and stroking it, and struggled to keep her face impassive.

The tight, well-worn jeans should have looked incongruous with the obviously expensive sweater, but they didn't—any more than the luxury car had looked incongruous outside what appeared to be just another waterfront dive. Daniel was apparently comfortable with both inconsistencies, perhaps not recognising them as inconsistencies at all, and therefore they seemed natural.

'I hope you're hungry.' He pushed the inner door open and guided Holly through with a hand lightly pressed against her back. A wave of intoxicating aromas filled her nostrils and prompted a Pavlovian rumble in her stomach; but that sensory assault was overwhelmed by the feel of his hand on her back. Obviously, the sweater wasn't thick enough. It was no defence at all.

The lobster dinners made his most lavish praise seem a gross understatement, and the restaurant would for ever be one of Holly's favourites.

Totally unpretentious, with scuffed wooden floors, battered sea lamps, and a collection of antique potbellied stoves, Holly couldn't help but think it was the kind of place Robert would have loved. Wisely, she kept that thought to herself, and concentrated solely on enjoying the company at hand.

Unexpectedly, Daniel was making that easy. He was perfectly at home here, obviously an old friend of most of the staff. There were many hearty greetings, eyebrows raised at Holly with such exaggerated outlandishness that even she had to laugh, and a generous spirit of conviviality that was every bit as warming as the endless flow of icy beer.

From behind her mug she watched, fascinated, as this sombre man came alive in the company of what she soon realised were his friends. He bantered with the help, teasing the girls mercilessly, laughing aloud so often that Holly began to wonder what had ever made her think he was too serious. His eyes were alight now, brilliantly blue, and his smile slashed the darkness of his face in a benevolent white curve that stopped her breath when she looked at it. His hair seemed to respond to the mood of its owner, tumbling across his forehead in total disarming array. Staring at the black curls completely out of control, she thought for the first time that he looked very, very young.

'All right, I give up,' she said finally, smiling at him across the heaped ruins of one of the best meals she'd ever eaten. 'Who are you, anyway?'

His grin was artless, and somehow it was connected to her pulse, making it race whenever he turned it on her. 'I am Daniel Chesterfield: gloomy, solitary, heartless, feared and hated columnist, destroyer emeritus, Prince of Darkness to some, or so I hear.' Outrageously, he winked at her. 'Except here. Here, I'm just Dan.'

'Then this is where you should always be,' she said softly.

He inclined his head slightly, then sipped from his mug, eyeing her steadily over the rim. 'Ridiculous outfit notwithstanding, you're a spectacularly beautiful woman, you know. I suppose you get tired of hearing that.'

'Oh, I do,' she countered quickly, flushing with embarrassment. 'I do, indeed. People stopping me on the street all the time, telling me just how beautiful I am . . . it's very tiring.' She covered her eyes with one hand in a dramatic gesture, and then frowned, sobering instantly, staring into the past, into her image of herself—an image created in part by Robert.

She was . . . cute. Gamine, perhaps, with a childlike innocence of expression that Robert had commented on time and again. But she wasn't beautiful. Never once had he accused her of that.

Suddenly it seemed imperative to know what Daniel saw when he looked at her.

'Why?' she demanded, almost crossly. 'Why do you think I'm . . .' even the word made her hesitate ' . . . beautiful?'

His smile quirked at a question he obviously thought strange. 'You're serious, aren't you? You

don't see yourself that way.' He shook his head,
mystified. 'All right, then——' He cocked his head
in mock appraisal and pretended to study her face
objectively, ticking off points on his fingers. 'First
of all, you have an incredibly sensuous
mouth—seductive, actually—and solemn, dark
eyes. They hardly ever lighten, you know, even
when you laugh, they still look so—wounded.' He
checked her expression to see if he'd offended her.
'A man could get lost in eyes like that. There's a
history in them, begging to be learned . . .'

Holly realised she was holding her breath, that
the mouth he had just described as sensual was
parted now, anticipating.

He leaned back in his chair and looked at her
through half closed eyes that made her tremble.
'But there are a lot of pretty women in New York.
It's the character in your face that sets it apart. A
kind of bravery. It balances the beauty, makes it
strong, gives it the kind of quality that will endure.
Understand?'

It felt as if she was shaking her head, but she
wasn't sure the command had ever completed the
circuit from brain to muscle. No. She didn't
understand. Who the hell was he describing?
Certainly not Robert's trusting, puppy-eyed
darling, the woman unscarred by life—and that
was who she was, after all. That was the woman
Robert had loved; the woman she had had to be.

Like a slow-motion film, he leaned forward
across the table, his hands circling the frosty
surface of his mug. 'I don't know anything about

you, Holly. Not where you came from, your childhood, your family . . . tell me. Tell me all of it.'

She looked down quickly, to find her hands twisting the paper napkin she held in her lap, reliving for the first time in a long time the pain she'd felt at the death of her parents. 'There's nothing much to tell,' she stammered. 'It's just a collection of happy times, and sad times, like everyone else's life.' She looked up with a wistful smile, surprised by the way he caught his breath, as if he had felt her pain. She forced her smile to broaden and exhaled mightily. 'I'll tell you about some of the happy times, if you like.'

She almost missed the nearly imperceptible lowering of his brows. 'Then you'd only be telling me half of the story. That isn't enough.'

Her shoulders sagged suddenly, as if the support that had been holding them up all these years had suddenly evaporated. Dear God! Half the story had always been enough for Robert. Any more than that would have been too much. How he'd hated it when she'd voiced her frustrations aloud, or permitted even a passing sadness to show! He couldn't abide the acknowledgement that sorrow or suffering existed in the world, and certainly not in the woman he loved. It simply didn't fit in with the rosy way he looked at life. He'd brushed any unhappy subject away with a kind of fearful impatience. 'Let's not dwell on the unpleasant, Holly,' he'd told her. 'Let's just think happy thoughts.'

Suddenly a tidal wave of all the things Robert hadn't known about her; hadn't wanted to know, swelled up inside with a pressure that demanded release. She began hesitantly, touching lightly on the tragedy of her parents' death, exposing in tiny snatches the underbelly of her vulnerability, as if it were something to be ashamed of. Yes, dammit, her mind cried out as her voice droned on passively, there were times when life was hard, when I was miserable, when grief and exhaustion and struggle coloured every day, and depression almost overwhelmed me. Dammit, Robert! Why didn't you want to know that part of me? You can't do away with the bad parts of life just by pretending they don't exist . . .

But that was what Robert had done.

The realisation struck her, stopped her in mid-sentence, took her breath away. Who had Robert loved? *What* had Robert loved? Some cardboard, two-dimensional pretence of a woman with a smiling face that never showed pain? A shallow, empty mind that locked the door on any emotion that was remotely serious, and perpetuated a charade of constant, mindless joy?

Daniel watched the sudden, stunning oppression creep across her face, leaving it colourless. Tentatively, his hand reached across the table and covered hers. She glanced down at their hands, her eyes glazed, and without realising it curled her fingers around his palm.

CHAPTER EIGHT

SOBERED by the sudden, brutal insight that made Robert's gay, light-hearted charm seem somehow sinister, Holly became pensive and quiet. That innate ability of Robert's to see only the good, to feel only joy—all that time she'd thought of it as a gift, when what it had really been was a weakness. Her image of Robert began to crumble, like a plaster statue exposed too long to the elements, and that subtle, insidious collapse of what she had believed him to be almost destroyed her.

Daniel never questioned her change of mood, but simply paid the bill and guided her gently from the warmth of the restaurant to the bitter, oppressive chill of the waterfront in winter.

Mindlessly she allowed him to tuck her hand into the crook of his elbow, to lead her down the damp, dark streets in a measured walk that enhanced the process of thought. The mournful call of a distant foghorn echoed and re-echoed among the sodden, sorry collection of ramshackle buildings whose prime had long passed. Occasionally they came upon the last vestiges of a dirty pile of white, testament to the fact that even snow could not blanket the meanness of the docks. Only the sea ruled here.

Holly took immeasurable comfort from Daniel's strong presence at her side, and only when her legs began to complain did she realise that they had been walking for a very long time, in complete silence. She stopped under the faint glow of one of the few streetlights that painted faded yellow circles on the ground, and looked up at him.

'You haven't said a word since we left the restaurant.'

The smooth suede of his glove cradled one side of her face in an exquisitely tender gesture. 'I didn't want to intrude.'

'On what?'

Never would she have expected to see such understanding in those eyes. 'You needed time to be sad.'

Her brows tipped, then she dropped her head and started to walk again, back towards the resturant and the car.

Time to be sad, she mused. He didn't even know what she was sad about, only that she was, and that time to ponder such things was important.

Unconsciously, she moved closer to him, tucking her hand more firmly into his arm, matching her stride to his.

The man that rounded the corner just ahead seemed more like a mirage than reality on the deserted waterfront. As they drew closer, Holly saw that he was old, hunched into a thin, frayed jacket, his unshaven face pale and drawn with the sallowness that usually accompanied a debilitating illness.

An umittened hand snaked out of his pocket as they approached, gnarled, arthritic fingers curled over the upward plam. 'Gotta dollar, Mr Chesterfield?' he whined, stepping directly in front of them. 'Gotta dollar for the needy?'

Even as Holly felt her eyes fill with compassion, she felt a current of tension ripple through the muscles of Daniel's arm. 'The restaurant still needs a busboy,' he growled. 'Go work for your dollar.'

The old man's eyes widened guilelessly as he waved one clawlike hand in front of Daniel's face. 'Can't work. No, sir. Can't work. Not since the arthritis. Gotta dollar, then? Gotta dollar for a poor soul who can't earn his own bread?'

'Get lost,' Daniel's voice rasped as he pushed the old man to one side.

Holly was so shocked by his display of heartlessness that she followed beside him automatically for a few steps before she remembered to act. 'But Daniel . . .' She snatched at his sleeve to pull him back. 'Look at him! He's poor, and sick, and . . .'

With a roughness that startled her, he grabbed her arm and jerked her forward like a recalcitrant child.

'Daniel!' she shouted, dragging her heels. 'It's only a dollar, for God's sake!'

She jerked her arm free and spun on the path, digging in her pocket for a dollar of her own, but when she looked up the old man had disappeared. 'Where did he go?' she whispered.

'Home. Which is where we're going.'

She glared up at him, then jammed her hands in her pockets and strode purposefully away. He had to lengthen his stride to keep up with her. 'He was pathetic,' she muttered, infuriated by Daniel's callousness, staring straight ahead, refusing to look at him, still seeing the face of the old man. 'How could you turn him away like that? How could you refuse to help another human being in trouble? And what would it have cost you? A dollar! A lousy dollar!'

'You're out of line, Holly,' he warned her, but she refused to listen.

'That's what's wrong with the world, you know! There are too many people like you in it! People who won't spare a minute or a dime for others who haven't been so fortunate, like that poor man back there! Well, thank God there are *some* willing to give a little, like . . .'

She stopped dead, sucking in her breath sharply.

'Like dear, departed Robert?' he finished her sentence scornfully. He grabbed her by the shoulders and spun her to face him. For some reason she couldn't begin to imagine, *he* looked furious with *her*. 'I'll just bet he always had a spare dollar to press into some grimy hand before he went on his merry way, didn't he?'

Holly stared up at him, her mouth open in surprise. He'd said it like an accusation, and that didn't make sense. Robert *had* always been overtly generous, an unwitting target for any tramp that came along; and he'd always been quick to press money into upturned palms without a second thought. What could possibly be wrong with that? He may have wobbled a bit on her mental pedestal tonight, but his compassion for his fellow man was limitless, and you certainly couldn't fault him for his generosity.

He shook her memory away with one hard jerk on her shoulders. 'Well, I'm not Robert,' he hissed down at her, and she noticed with alarm that his eyes had darkened again. 'I'm not remotely like him, thank God, and if that's what you're hoping to find, if that's what you really think you want, then get the hell out of my life!'

Holly's mouth dropped open in mute surprise. How had they got from the argument about the old man to whether or not Daniel was like Robert? She would have asked him that, but he was already striding angrily away through the empty streets, leaving her behind as the first flakes of the night's snow began to drift downward.

Baffled, she looked at her dismal surroundings, shrugging as if to share her confusion with an unseen audience, and then she noticed the deep pockets of darkness between the old buildings, the ominous silence of a street where no one walked alone.

'Daniel?' she called timidly, racing after the echo of his angry footsteps, her cape blowing open behind her.

She jumped into the car just as he started the engine, and turned towards him, still breathing hard. 'You would have left me here!' she accused him.

He slammed the gearshift down and stood on the accelerator, leaving twin scorchmarks of rubber on the pavement next to the kerb.

Alarmed, Holly braced one hand on the dashboard while she fumbled with the other for her seat-belt. Clearly, it was going to be a wild ride home.

Daniel's rage subsided during the long ride, as if the monotony of motorway driving had lulled him into a state that was at least more approachable, if not openly receptive.

While she pretended to peer past him at the wind-driven snow hitting his window, she was actually watching his face, warily assessing his changing mood.

Initially the sharp ridge of his clenched jaw had warned her to keep silent, as had his narrowed eyes, levelled with furious concentration on the road ahead. She didn't have to see those eyes head-on to know that they were navy blue, almost black.

Never in her life had she been in awe of a man's anger, and she had certainly never been silenced by it; but being silent now seemed less a matter of fear than one of respect. Perhaps he needed time to be angry, just as she had needed time to be sad. Besides, she was savouring the silence. It helped her to think, and his preoccupation with negotiating the slick road gave her a chance to study him at length, virtually unnoticed.

He certainly looked the part of a man who would turn his back on others in need, like that pathetic old man back there. There was a cruel cast to the sharply defined profile, enhanced now by the eerie glow reflected from the dashboard lights. The longer she studied him, the less likely it seemed that he had been related to Robert at all. Never, surely, had two brothers been so unalike. Was that why his hatred had survived the grave? Had it begun in childhood?

She imagined Daniel as a sombre, introspective child, forever taking a back seat to his brother's gregarious charm. Certainly Robert's affectionate, jolly nature would make him the favourite, and perhaps Daniel had always felt left out. It wouldn't be so surprising. Hadn't she read that sibling rivalry was one of man's fiercest, most competitive arenas? Perhaps Daniel was still competing with his brother, still trying to beat him at something, even after his death.

She caught her breath as the thought struck her. Had she become the prize? Was she nothing more to Daniel than the means by which he would finally win over Robert? And how would he measure his victory?

The answer sank into the mire of her thoughts, nearly pulling her down with it. Of course! She should have realised it before. He'd been perfectly frank about it. Holly had given herself to Robert in every way but one—physically—and if Daniel achieved that, he would have something Robert had never had. He would have beaten him at last.

Apparently he didn't notice her newly tense reserve as he walked her to the guest-house door, or if he did he put it down to the ugly scene back at the waterfront.

His voice was controlled, his face calm as he took her key and fitted it into the lock. 'I think I'd better come in.'

'Why?' She tried not to sound panicked, but now, more than ever, his motives were suspect.

He pushed past her and flicked the switch that turned on a small lamp near the fireplace. 'Because letting you cling to your delusions has turned out to be more expensive than I'd anticipated. It's time you heard the truth about Robert, if you've got the stomach for it.'

She bristled slightly, following him inside, closing the door hard behind her. 'Fine. And after you tell me your truth, I'll tell you mine. I'm sure they're quite different. I don't think you knew your brother at all.'

His lips curved into a derisive smile as he turned his eyes on her. They were coldly expressionless. 'I knew him better than anyone on earth,' he said flatly, 'but as a courtesy, I'll listen to what you have to say. Get us some drinks. I have the feeling we'll need them.'

There was a respectable fire crackling in the hearth by the time she returned to the living-room with a bottle of wine and two glasses. Daniel was crouched before it, intent on the precise positioning of one particular log. The firelight danced across his profile, making it seem more sinister than ever.

As she sank to lotus position on the floor, the coffee-table safely between them, he spun on the balls of his feet without rising, his arms braced on his thighs, his hands dangling between his legs. The fire behind him surrounded his head with an unearthly, golden glow, but his face was in complete shadow. She heard a sound that might have been a chuckle, and knew by the movements of his head that he was amused that she had chosen to sit behind the barrier of the coffee-table. He rose lithely to his feet, filled both glasses, then lifted the coffee-table and set it aside. He handed her one glass, set his on the brick hearth, then reclined on his side, facing her, one elbow propped to hold his head. There was no longer anything between them.

She took a large swallow of wine and felt the back of her neck prickle. 'Well, go ahead. You were going to tell me the truth about Robert.' She kept her voice coldly formal, which seemed ridiculous with him sprawled so casually on the floor.

He lifted his glass slightly, and she was suddenly glad the shadows obscured his expression. 'Ladies first, by all means. You think you knew him so well? Then tell me. Tell me all about my brother. Tell me why you loved the bastard.'

If his tone had been just slightly less contemptuous; if his posture hadn't been so insolently self-confident; if only he hadn't called Robert a bastard; she might have held back. But he wasn't only attacking a man she had loved, he was attacking a man no longer able to defend himself. That in itself was despicable, even cowardly, and her anger flared to the surface. It would serve him right to be forced to listen to what a wonderful person Robert had really been; and if the implication was that Daniel was inferior by comparison, well then, that was just the way things were.

She was troubled briefly by the thought that what she would say would be painful for him to hear, but then she remembered that she was nothing more than a prize in a competition with a dead man, and spite urged her onward. Since she couldn't really see his face anyway, she looked straight into the fire, letting it hypnotise her, letting it carry her back to that day two years before, when she'd first met Robert . . .

'It was only two weeks before Christmas,' she began, 'and yet everything seemed ugly. Shabby and mean-spirited. I'd decided to do some shopping after work, and I guess I'd hoped that I'd rediscover the Christmas spirit somewhere in the streets of Manhattan. That was pretty naïve, I suppose, but New York is supposed to shine at Christmas, isn't it? Anyway, if the decorations were pretty, I didn't see them; I only saw the commercialism, the garishness. And if there were loving, generous people on the streets that day, I didn't see them, either; I only saw crowds of hurrying, angry shoppers, begrudging every dime they spent on gifts they didn't want to buy for people they didn't like. That's what Christmas had become for me in the years since my parents had died; in a way, that's what the world had become.' She took a sip of wine and shrugged. 'The joy was gone, and Christmas itself seemed such a hypocrisy. There wasn't any of that goodwill towards men they drum into your head when you're a child. I couldn't see it anywhere . . . until I saw Robert.'

A slow, almost beatific smile touched her face with a glow that did not come entirely from the firelight. 'You know what he was doing?'

'I shudder to think.'

Holly went on as if she hadn't heard the sarcasm in his voice.

'He was standing right in front of the biggest department store in New York City, grinning like a crazy man, grabbing passers-by and shaking their hands, even hugging some of them, wishing them Merry Christmas in a voice you could hear over all the bells and buses and horns—and the most remarkable thing . . .' she caught her lower lip between her teeth and frowned, as if she still couldn't believe it had ever happened '. . . the most remarkable thing was the way all those angry, stern-faced people responded to him. He was like a rock in the middle of some dark, boiling river that wasn't so dark any more, once it passed him. You could draw a line in the crowd where Robert was standing. Sombre people on one side; smiling people on the other. It was almost a magic thing, the way he touched all those strangers, if only for an instant. I guess it was the first time I has ever really understood how much power one person has to make another person happy, if you can only find the courage to reach out, and I think I wanted to be close to that kind of power for ever.'

'Was he passing out money?' Daniel asked contemptuously.

'Money?' Holly's eyes shifted impatiently and her expression hardened. 'No. He was passing out something much more important on that day. But there were times, a lot of times, when he gave money away, too; and sacks of gifts we'd take to the children's hospital, and to the poorer sections of town . . . places where you would certainly never go, making friends of people you would hurry past on the street.' Now it was Holly's voice that was contemptuous. 'Like the old man we met tonight, for instance. Robert would have helped him. Robert helped anyone who needed it, without question. He made friends everywhere he went; he made strangers his family; and for the first time since my parents died, when I was with Robert, I had a family too. I wasn't alone any more. Robert didn't just make me believe in love again; he made me believe in . . .' she shrugged with the frustration of searching for the proper way to say it ' . . . *man,* I guess. The goodness in all men. How could I possibly help but love anyone who had shown me that?'

'How indeed?' Daniel murmured, and Holly heard the sarcasm in his tone.

'It wasn't just me,' she said angrily. 'Everybody loved Robert. You were his brother. Surely you knew that?'

He sighed and eased up to a lotus position that mirrored her own, turning just enough towards the fire so she could see how bitter his smile was. 'Nobody knows it better.'

'But . . . then you *do* understand . . .'

He looked at her quietly. 'Of course I understand. I've always understood. You're the one who doesn't. Yes, everybody who met Robert loved him, almost instantly. That was the nature of his charm. The problem was that he just couldn't love anybody back.'

In spite of the earnestness of his tone, Holly didn't for a moment consider what he said seriously. 'That's ridiculous!' She dismissed the notion with a wave of her hand. 'Robert loved the whole world.'

Daniel remained motionless, but for a slight nod. 'Exactly.'

Holly frowned at him impatiently. It was clear that he was driving at something, or perhaps guiding her gently to what he thought was an obvious conclusion. She just couldn't imagine what it was. 'What are you trying to say?'

'You've already said it,' he told her, and she was more disturbed by the unexpected kindness in his tone than she would have been by disdain. 'He loved everybody. That's a very safe, impersonal kind of love, you know. It's easy, compared to the responsibility of loving some people more than others. Robert was incapable of that kind of commitment.'

'That's not true! He loved *me!*'

'Of course he did, you little fool!' he shouted, spinning towards her so his face was in shadow again. 'And why shouldn't he? You fed his fantasy of being the semi-divine man who loved the world! But you didn't love him—not like a normal woman loves a normal man—you *adored* him! There's a hell of a difference!'

Holly jumped to her feet furiously, her hands tightened at her sides in balls of rage. Daniel shot up to face her, almost at the same moment.

'You don't know anything!' she shouted. 'You don't know the first thing about the kind of love Robert was capable of, or what was between us!'

'The hell I don't!' He grabbed her shoulders and shook her. 'I know that if Robert had been capable of *normal* love . . . the kind of love that's *supposed* to happen between men and women . . . he would have had you in his bed long before he died! And yet he didn't, did he? How the hell do you suppose he managed that? How the hell do you suppose he managed to keep his hands off you for the year you knew each other? I didn't even love you, and given half the chance I would have taken you the night we met!'

She stopped struggling instantly and looked up at him, her breath caught in her throat.

For a long moment, there was only the sound of the fire and the whisper of a cold wind at the windows.

Holly felt like she was teetering on the brink of a great precipice, about to embrace an understanding that would shatter her image of Robert, the beauty of the memories Robert had given her. She took a quick mental step backward, away from the abyss, but made no attempt to move from beneath Daniel's hands.

"It's ironic, isn't it?' His voice jarred the silence and made her jump. 'The thing you admired most about Robert—his blanket love for all of mankind

—was the very quality that made it impossible for him to give you, or anyone, the kind of individual love they deserved . . .'

She broke away from him at last, rubbing her shoulders as if she could erase the feel of his hands. 'No! You're wrong! You never understood him, that's all! You think that because your own capacity for love is so limited, that *everyone's* is! That's like saying a piano can't be played, simply because you can't play it!'

Her shout reverberated in the little room, sounding just a little bit desperate. They stood less than a foot from each other in the flickering light, Holly trembling with the force of the emotions that ran through her, Daniel tensed, his hands lifted slightly towards her as if he expected her to fall. She clenched her teeth and struggled to regain control, frantic to turn the conversation away from the introspection that kept dragging her back to the brink of that terrible hole. If she faltered now, she knew instinctively that Robert—the love of Robert that had sustained her—would tumble into the hole with her, and shatter into a million pieces at the bottom. Robert had shown her the world as it could be—a placed filled with love and under-standing and a million strangers who could be friends, if only she' reached out to them. But, if Robert himself had been a lie, then didn't it follow that all the rest was a lie, too? And, if that were the case, then she would be alone again.

Daniel was watching her face carefully, as if he could read the frantic thoughts behind it. 'You've

thought about it, haven't you?' he asked softly.
'And it bothered you. You never quite understood
that pure, pristine spiritual love of his. You
couldn't have. Not with your appetites.'

'Stop it!' she hissed, spinning away from him,
hugging her elbows close to her body, warding off
a deadly chill that had nothing to do with
temperature. Damn him, damn him, he was right.
How many times had she asked herself what was
wrong with her, because she had wanted more than
Robert had been ready to give? And there *had* been
something wrong, because he had given her his
heart, his spirit . . . how petty could she be, to have
all that, and still hunger for something as base, as
inconsequential, as physical gratification?

'That was my failing, not his,' she said softly,
turning to face him. Light from the fire danced
across her face, and Daniel sucked in a pained
breath, as if something in her expression had
wounded him. 'You'll have to do better than that
to make me hate him.' She looked up at him with
quiet, resigned expectation. 'Well? What are you
waiting for? You came in here to tell me the truth
about Robert, to tell me why you hated him.
Presumably with the intention of making me hate
him, too. So, go ahead. I'm listening.'

He looked at her expressionlessly for a moment.
'Maybe I was wrong.' The words sounded
constricted, as if they'd been dragged through a
narrow passageway then flung to the earth,
flattened and limp. 'Maybe you didn't know
Robert, but maybe what you thought he was was

enough.' One side of his mouth lifted in a tired smile. 'I won't take that away from you, Holly. I wouldn't do that for the world.'

"Wait a minute . . .' she started to say, but he was already moving swiftly to the door, and then out into the softly falling snow. She watched through the window as he plodded heavily towards the house, his head down, his hands shoved deep into the pockets of his jeans.

CHAPTER NINE

HOLLY sat by the phone the next morning, waiting for the furious call to get over to the big house and get to work. She needed the summons, somehow feeling that, after last night, she no longer had the right to approach him without permission. And, more than that, she needed to hear anger in his voice, as if that would erase the defeat she had seen in him when he'd last left her.

At mid-morning she heard the rumble of his sports car leaving the drive, sighed with a despair she didn't quite understand, and looked for any available diversion.

She scrubbed and polished everything in the guest-house she could find to scrub or polish, forced herself to read three chapters of a book she found tedious, and puttered the rest of the morning away in the kitchen. She was desperate with boredom, frustrated by the unexpected ending to their conversation the night before, and driven now by a curiosity she could no longer contain.

At noon she gave in to the almost desperate need to see another human being, and called Jeanine to arrange a late lunch in the city . . .

'You look tired, honey.' Jeanine frowned at her across the crisp linen and crystal of the Rosewood

Room, her brow creased with concern. She was a tall, large-boned woman, saved from the appearance of coarseness by an inbred grace that made her slightest move seem delicate. There was nothing delicate about her spirit, however. She was a strong-willed partner for Hampton, fiercely loyal, and uncompromisingly honest. 'Is that Daniel working you too hard? Being difficult, as always?'

Holly's smile felt worn, as if she'd been using it too often with no real substance behind it. At the moment, Daniel was the enemy threatening to destroy her adoring memories of Robert, and yet it still pleased her, for some reason, to hear the affection in Jeanine's voice when she mentioned his name. 'You're very fond of him, aren't you Jeanine? You and Hampton both.'

'Of course we are. We've known Daniel since he was a baby. And loved him that long too, I suppose.'

'And yet you never mentioned him, and I never saw him at any of those fabulous parties you gave . . .'

Jeanine chuckled and tucked a greying curl of black hair behind her ear. 'Daniel's never been the party type, and friendship with him has always been sort of like membership in a secret club. Actually, we see quite a lot of him, but only alone. He isn't what you'd call a people person.' She smiled at her own understatement.

'Not like Robert.'

Jeanine's kind brown eyes sharpened slightly, and Holly saw something in them she didn't like.

'Well?' she prodded. 'You must have known Robert just as well, yet you never talked about him either. Not even when I was seeing him.'

Jeanine cleared her throat and patted nervously at the corner of her mouth with a napkin. 'We didn't really see that much of Robert, dear. As a matter of fact, I don't think he cared for our company. Not that that wasn't perfectly understandable, of course. We were his parents' friends, originally. A different generation entirely. It's no wonder he didn't . . .'

'You didn't like him, did you, Jeanine?' Holly held her breath while Jeanine looked at her, considering her answer.

'Hampton and I both knew how you felt about Robert, Holly. Never for a moment would we have considered saying anything against him. Then, or now.'

Holly leaned back in her chair and filled her cheeks with a frustrated puff of air. 'I have to know the truth about Robert, Jeanine. There's something there . . . something Daniel won't tell me, and we can't get past it.'

The older woman's face sagged helplessly, then tensed. 'I'm sorry, Holly. If you're looking for information about Robert—other than what you know, of course—then you're going to have to get it from Daniel. He's the only one who has the right to say anything.'

For the next week, Holly and Daniel never spoke of Robert, and yet in some ways she felt his presence by omission was almost more pervasive than it had been when she and Daniel had fought about him.

At least the work schedule had resumed, more gruelling than ever, and for that she was grateful. Every hour they worked together was one less hour she would have to spend alone, and her time alone was beginning to take on a nightmarish quality. She found herself recalling titbits of her time with Robert, remembering things about him that had seemed slightly eccentric then, but were more disturbing in retrospect. Like the time they went to the children's hospital.

With a money source that seemed inexhaustible, and a generosity of spirit to match, he had purchased scores of gifts—toys, clothes, books, dolls—hauled them all to the hospital, then dropped them off at the main desk. 'But don't you want to give them to the children yourself?' the administrator had asked, giving voice to Holly's own thoughts. Robert had declined with a stammering graciousness she had taken for modesty at the time, but was that really all it had been, or was there another reason he wouldn't go into the wards?

And how about the money he sent to the families evicted from that rundown tenement? He'd *mailed* that—great wads of cash in plain white envelopes with no return address. 'Wouldn't you like to give it to them personally, Robert?' she'd asked him. 'Maybe help them find new places to live, get to know the people you're helping?' He'd shamed her by replying gently that he liked to remain anony-

mous, that their gratitude would embarrass him. It
seemed a reasonable answer—for a saint. As for
Holly, admittedly *not* a saint, she had wanted
desperately to involve herself personally, to see the
changes a simple gift of kindness could produce;
but that had been a selfish motive, Robert had
pointed out. She had to learn to be satisfied with
the act of giving itself. That was supposed to be
enough.

'I never could get the hang of being *that* selfless,'
she chuckled aloud, remembering.

'What?'

Her smile faded instantly and her expression
stiffened. For a moment, she'd forgotten where she
was, the memories had been so strong. She forced
herself to meet Daniel's eyes over the library table
where they'd been working. 'Sorry. Just talking to
myself.'

'No, you weren't.' He tapped the photograph
she was holding with the tip of his pencil. 'You
were talking to that picture, which is worse. You've
finally gone over the end, haven't you?'

She smiled easily, leaning back in the straight-
backed chair, extending her arms in a luxurious
stretch. It was the relaxed gesture of someone
perfectly at ease, a gesture she would never have
made in Daniel's presence a week ago. But, after
that night in the guest-house, there had been an
unspoken agreement between them to pretend, at
least in each other's company, that Robert had
never existed; and the longer they kept up the
pretence, the more relaxed their relationship

became. The constant tension of imminent conflict was gone and, much to the surprise of both, they discovered they were a remarkably effective team. The book had become as much a labour of love for Holly as it was for Daniel, and their progress to date was considerable. They had dealt only with the photos Daniel had selected, of course—to avoid trouble, Holly had postponed demanding that the pictures Robert had chosen be included in the book. The issue would have to be faced eventually, but there was no need to hurry catastrophe, as Hampton always said.

'So?' Daniel prodded, his eyes smiling. 'What were you muttering?'

He was particularly appealing tonight, his hair mussed from running his fingers through it, his eyes drooping lazily from lack of sleep. It was one of those rare moments when he looked almost harmless.

Holly ignored the question, lifted her hair off her neck, then shook her head to rearrange it. It fell in a cloud of golden brown over her shoulders.

'I wasn't muttering; I was praying. Praying for a boss who kept reasonably regular hours, who didn't keep me up until . . .' she glanced at her watch '. . . three o'clock in the morning.'

'Three o'clock? Good lord, I had no idea it was so late!' He leaned back complacently and balanced his chair on two legs, his hands laced over his stomach. 'It hardly seemed like work at all, the time passes so quickly.'

'Speak for yourself.'

'I always do; and in this instance, for you, too, I think.' Without a pause, he added, 'You were saying something about not being able to get the hang of selflessness. That word alone is a dead giveaway. You must have been thinking of Robert.'

Whatever peace that had existed between them shattered instantly, and Holly felt the old tension like an electric glove tightened around her heart. Why had he done that? He was the one who hadn't wanted Robert's name mentioned in the first place. Why did he have to be the one to bring it up and ruin everything?

She dropped her eyes, saw that her hands were grasping each other on the table, and put them quickly in her lap, out of sight. 'I can't believe you did that,' she whispered.

'What—mention the unmentionable? It's about time, isn't it?'

She found a loose thread in her sweater and began to coil it around her finger. 'I guess that depends on the reason.'

'For the book.' He affected nonchalance. 'It's time we pulled the photos we want to use out of Robert's box.'

Holly jerked her head up, her lips parted in the beginnings of a smile she was not prepared to complete just yet, in case it was premature. 'You want to include some of his photographs in the book?'

'First of all, they're not his photographs; they're mine. I took them. He just picked them out. And second of all, they belong in the book, those happy shots, just as much as the others. I knew that, of course, but my feelings for Robert kept me from admitting it. You were right about that much. So——' he smiled lazily, pleased with what he had said '—what did you mean, you could never get the hang of that kind of selflessness?'

And because he had spoken of Robert and hadn't exploded, she told him—about the children's hospital incident, and the the tenement families. In the telling, she denigrated her own desire for personal involvement, and elevated Robert's insistence on anonymity to nearly divine status.

'Oh, don't be an ass!' His words were clipped, but not angry, exactly. 'Of course he wouldn't go into the wards! Our Robert, voluntarily coming face to face with pain and suffering? Actually getting to *know* other people on a personal level? What a preposterous idea. Robert couldn't have handled such a dose of real life. Same thing for the tenement families. You must have scared the hell out of him, suggesting he actually get *involved*. Haven't you figured it out yet? Robert gave, and then ran—with his eyes closed, most of the time, so he wouldn't have to see anything ugly. But he never really gave himself—just smiles, and gifts, and money. That's all Robert had to give.'

Holly just sat here, flinching every now and then as if particular words were tiny, pointed missiles aimed at her face. Daniel was looking down as he talked, shuffling through a stack of photos, thinking nothing of what he was saying or the effect it might have on her. They were just words, after all. He had no way of knowing that she would connect them with a dozen memories of Robert, and see the beauty of those memories destroyed in the light he was shedding so casually.

It was all starting to make perfect, horrible sense . . . the way Robert pressed money into the palm of any beggar, perhaps not in the pure spirit of generosity, but *just to make them go away;* the way he embraced any stranger, but never, in all the time she had known him, had he followed through to make one of those strangers a friend. Had *that* been his idea of love for his fellow man? A quick coin and a fast farewell?

Ships passing in the night. That was what all of Robert's contacts had been. Except for her, of course. What about her? What had Robert really felt for her?

The question nearly tore her apart.

Nearly a week later, on a Sunday afternoon, Daniel suggested they put the book aside and take the evening off.

Holly, totally exhausted by the late hours they'd been keeping, threw her pencil down on the library table and cheered. 'At the risk of looking a gift horse in the mouth, what's come over you? You usually work me until I drop on Sundays.'

Daniel smiled at her. 'This is a special Sunday. The servants put up the Christmas tree this afternoon, and tonight there will be carollers. Traditionally . . .'

Holly groaned at yet another tradition.

'. . . traditionally,' Daniel continued, pointedly ignoring her, 'the Chesterfields spend the evening admiring the tree, listening to carols, and drinking some God-awful yuletide drink Anna forces on us.'

Holly put two fingers to her mouth and blinked absently.

'What's the matter?'

Her lips quivered a little. 'Nothing. Nothing at all. It's just that . . . I hadn't really thought about it before. I'll be spending Christmas here.'

'Well, of course you will. What of it?'

The smile touched her mouth so briefly that Daniel wasn't entirely sure it had ever been there at all.

Stop it, Holly, she commanded herself, feeling the stupid, stupid tears well up behind her eyes, but she couldn't stop it before one traitorous drop spilled on to her cheek and glistened there for a moment before she brushed at it furiously.

'Holly?' Daniel tensed, leaning over the table as if he intended to vault it and come to her aid.

'It's nothing.' She shook her head in embarrassment, waving away his concern, but her voice still faltered. 'It'll . . . just be nice . . . spending Christmas in a house . . . with other people. Like it used to be.'

'When your parents were alive,' he said softly, frowning so hard that his brows nearly touched over his nose. 'Well . . .' He pushed himself away from the table, brushed his hands together, and forced the brightest, falsest smile she'd seen on his face yet. How about that? Daniel Chesterfield wasn't as hard-hearted as he pretended to be. She'd actually touched him, drawn him into her own poignant, nostalgic emotion, and he was working very hard to make sure it didn't show. 'Well,' he repeated, 'you'd better get going, then. Anna's making a special supper, and you know how she gets when we're late. Wear something festive; something Christmassy. The carollers expect it of us, I'm afraid.' She was almost through the doorway when he called after her softly, 'Holly?'

She turned and looked down at him from the added height of the shallow steps.

'I'm glad you'll be here for Christmas.'

CHAPTER TEN

THE SERVANTS hadn't just 'put up a tree'; they'd given the entire front part of the house a sparkling seasonal facelift. Red velvet bows gathered pine garlands over the foyer's entry arch, and from there draped an entrance into the large, high-ceiled living-room. The room's pastels were pushed into the background of baskets of polished balls and crystal bowls of holly. Great masses of bright red poinsettias clustered on every surface, and nearly a hundred candles filled the room with their magic, flickering light.

The tree stood in the far corner, a tower of fragrant green, with literally hundreds of tiny gold lights, and nearly as many red and gold ornaments, pefectly placed to reflect the candles like colourful mirrors.

The scene was heart-stoppingly beautiful, and Holly caught her breath when she walked in from the dining-room, one hand pressed lightly to her chest.

'I felt exactly the same way when I saw you tonight,' Daniel said at her side, taking her arm and guiding her to a Queen Anne love-seat flanking the fireplace.

Holly blushed at the compliment, but made no

attempt to parry it. This night, unlike the last time she'd been in this room, she hadn't dressed for guests—for the approval of unknown strangers. She'd dressed for Christmas. And for Daniel.

Her dress was a draped red taffeta with narrow green stripes, entirely too gay for any occasion but one, and for as long as she lived she would associate the rustle of its floor-length skirt with Christmas. She'd first worn it on the last Christmas she had spent with her parents, and she'd worn it every year since, even alone in the brownstone. She smiled a little, thinking that a Sherwood could have traditions, too. The full sleeves billowed about her arms, caught at the wrist with French cuffs in the same snowy linen that framed the scooped *décolletage*. A large sash cinched tight against her already tiny waist, and tied into a large bow at the back. It was a dress right out of *Little Women,* and it belonged in this room on this occasion.

In keeping with the dress, she had clasped her hair into an intricate coil at the nape of her neck, leaving just a few tendrils to curl at her ears and over her forehead. An almost childish locket with a single red stone lay just above her breasts, quivering and catching the light whenever she breathed.

'From Robert?' Daniel had asked her over dinner.

'My father,' she'd answered quietly.

As they settled on to the love-seat together, Holly clasped her hands together in her lap, like a child who could hardly contain her excitement. 'This is a fairyland!' she murmured, entranced by the candles, the tree, the tang of aromatic pine.

'You're surprised.'

She hesitated, then nodded vigorously. 'I think I imagined you as some sort of Scrooge, holed up in your cheerless office during the Christmas season, counting lumps of coal, bah-humbugging everyone.'

Daniel tipped his head back and laughed soundlessly. 'I might have been like that . . . lord knows, I'm too serious most of the time. But Mother wouldn't have it. She loved Christmas, and everything that went with it. This . . .' his gesture encompassed the room '. . . is her doing. She forced the holiday on us all, until finally we got used to it. Now I can't imagine it any other way.'

Some of the excitement left Holly's face as she realised that Daniel missed his parents—his mother, at least—as much as she missed hers. They were both without family, and never is the loss more keenly felt than during a season that traditionally brings families together.

We share that, at least, she thought, turning to smile at him. If nothing else, we have in common the lingering sorrow of old grief.

Daniel looked every inch the aristocrat, dressed to receive company. His hair echoed the black of his dinner-jacket, and was, for once, properly directed off his forehead. Impulsively, Holly plucked a stem of holly from a table arrangement and tucked it into his lapel.

'There.' She patted his chest, much as a wife would pat her husband after fixing his tie, assuring him that he was presentable at last. 'Now you look festive.'

Anna scowled pointedly at the sprig of holly when she came in, bearing on a silver tray matching cups, engraving with an ornate 'C', filled to the brim with a frothy cream sprinkled with brown spice.

'Oh, Anna, it smells wondeful!' Holly scooped up a cup happily, forgetting for a moment that Anna had never wavered in her open dislike of her. 'What is it? A toddy?'

'It's deadly, that's what it is,' Daniel grumbled as he reached for his cup. 'I don't know why we can't have a brandy after dinner, like we usually do.'

'Because it's *Christmas,*' Holly and Anna said simultaneously, both clearly taken aback that they could share any sentiment, let alone voice it in unison. Holly just looked bewildered; Anna left the room in a huff.

'Christmas is a full week away,' Daniel reminded her, making a face at his first sip.

'But this is a special night, part of the Chesterfield tradition. You said so yourself.'

He nodded begrudgingly, licking a lace of foam from his upper lip. Holly reached in her pocket for the compulsory lace hankie, then reached over to dab at the corners of his mouth. It was an astounding thing for her to do, and yet somehow, at this moment, in this room, on this night, it seemed natural.

He grabbed her wrist gently, then pressed his lips to her upturned palm. He never took his eyes from hers, and Holly worried that he would feel the pounding of her pulse beneath his fingers. 'I haven't touched you in a long time,' he murmured, his breath collecting in her palm like a living mass of heat, 'but I haven't stopped wanting you. And at this moment, I want you more than I have ever wanted anything in my life.'

Holly was too helpless to speak, to move, even to breathe.

'Say it.' His eyes crackled with an intensity that made the rich blue fade to ice, but his voice was little more than a groan. 'You want the same thing. So say it aloud.' His hand tightened on her wrist, pulling her upper body towards him, and Holly knew that in the next instant, she wouldn't have to say anything at all.

Just as her breasts rose with the last gasp of a swimmer about to go under, a sound made them both freeze, mouths mere inches apart, eyes closing. Holly's senses were so heightened that she could almost imagine the feathery tips of her nerve-endings erect and quivering, waiting for his touch. She thought it might be almost physically painful, like a sudden burn.

The faint strains of young voices barely filtered through the rush of blood in her ears, then grew steadily louder. Daniel's eyes fell closed, he expelled a great, shaky breath, then dropped her wrist.

'The carollers are here.'

'I know,' she whispered, barely moving her lips. 'I hear them.'

As if following an inner command they both heard, they rose as one, straightened clothing that only felt as if it had been disturbed, and glided across the room to the bay windows with the grace of a couple who have been together for a very long time.

Holly followed Daniel's lead and raised a gracious hand to the group of young people clustered outside the window. 'I feel like mistress of the house,' she murmured.

'Then that's what you are.'

She stole a sideways glance up at him, but his eyes were fixed on the group outside, and the smile he wore was for their benefit. To Holly, it seemed almost paternal.

The front garden seemed almost a stage, constructed as a backdrop for this one performance. Artistically placed floodlights peeped through the snow, illuminating the frosty pines with a golden glow that reflected in the bright eyes of nearly twenty children. Holly couldn't help but think how strange it was to find so many in a neighbourhood such as this. Families able to afford the extravagant estates that lined this street were usually past child-bearing age.

And yet there was the proof, a cluster of rosy, innocent faces, from toddlers to teenagers, shining out from the dark wrappings of winter scarves and hats.

Suddenly the heart-rendingly sweet soprano of a young boy lifted and soared with such clarity of tone that Holly felt her throat tighten with emotion.

The other children joined in a harmonic chorus, poignant in its imperfection, and Holly, touched by something very close to rapture, reached for Daniel's hand and squeezed it hard and tried to keep her eyes dry.

The children sang several carols, ending with a rousing version of 'Deck the Halls' that was so enthusiastically sung, so happily, unashamedly joyous that Holly grinned from beginning to end. When the last tones died away, she turned to Daniel, and saw that his expression mirrored her own. His eyes crinkled at the corners with the force of his smile. She barely recognised him.

'Weren't they marvellous?' He leaned his head towards her, still clapping and smiling out at the children.

'Oh, they were better than that . . . Oh, no! Are they leaving?'

'Of course not!' he called happily as he stalked towards the entryway. 'They're coming in.'

Holly hiked up her skirts and skittered after him, skidding to a halt on the tile floor when she saw Anna already holding the front door wide, her dour face fairly alight with a broad smile. Holly barely recognised her, either.

Stunned, she watched dozens of snowy boots track across the immaculately buffed floor, and even as she was waiting for Anna's sharp admonition to ring out she heard a chorus of childish, excited voices greeting Anna and Daniel by name. The youngest girl, wobbling in stiff, snow-encrusted leggings, lifted her arms to Anna, and the old lady actually picked up the child and swung her high, then hugged her, snow and all, to her meagre bosom.

It's a miracle, that's what it is, Holly thought, mesmerised by the scene. Anything that makes old sour-faced Anna act like this *has* to be a miracle.

The children's chaperon was a round-faced jolly woman in a plain brown coat who stayed in the background during the first flurry of the children's greetings, then moved in to take charge. Her voice was brisk, her tone no-nonsense, but her face was kindly. It was clear that she loved the children, each and every one, and it was equally clear that they all returned the sentiment. 'Off with your boots, now, and all the rest of your things, or no egg nog, and no treats, and no introduction to the beautiful new lady.'

She beamed at Holly as she bent to help one of the younger children with her boots. 'We'll never be properly introduced at this rate,' she chuckled up at her, jerking her head to the eager mob that surrounded Daniel and Anna. 'I don't imagine the children will give them a moment's peace for some time to come. They wait all year for this, you know.'

She grunted when a stubborn boot finally relinquished its hold and rose slowly, pressing her hands to the small of her back with a grimace of relief, then holding one out to Holly. 'I'm Marcy Booth, guardian to this unruly bunch for the night. You must be Holly Sherwood. Daniel's told me a lot about you. You're every bit as pretty as he said you were.'

Taken aback that Daniel had told anyone about her, let alone that she was pretty, Holly hesitated for a moment before walking headlong into the confusion of boots and coats and little squirming bodies. She shook Marcy's callused, outstretched hand, met warm, brown eyes that she liked very much, then was distracted by a tug on her dress.

'I can't do the zipper.' A tiny, pudgy face frowned up at her. 'Can you do my zipper?'

Holly knelt to the floor, her dress flowering around her, feeling a tender rush of warmth to be so suddenly accepted. 'I have trouble doing zippers, too,' she said solemnly, pretending intense concentration on the little girl's coat. 'Maybe we can do it together.'

Marcy watched the pair with lively interest until the little girl, coatless at last, scooted away. 'You're very good with children,' she told Holly. 'Have any of your own?'

'I'm beginning to wish I had,' Holly answered absently, her eyes on the little girl as she ran after Anna down the hall towards the kitchen.

'Good.' Marcy brushed her hands together with satisfaction, as if she'd just solved a problem that had been troubling her for a long time. 'This house has been empty for too long.'

Holly frowned and opened her mouth to ask what on earth that had to do with her, but at that moment a speedy bundle of pure energy crashed into the shock absorber of her voluminous skirt with an impact that nearly knocked her over.

'Here, here, now!' Marcy scolded, clapping her hands, but Holly only laughed, captured the little blonde girl in a swooping embrace, and lifted her up to eye-level, thinking how wonderfully warm and alive the house felt with so many voices filling the emptiness.

For the next two hours the echoing spaces of the Chesterfield house reverberated with the joyous sounds of children. In blustering, excited groups, they exclaimed at the beauty of the living-room, periodically visited an enormous buffet Anna had set up in the dining-room, then scattered through the house like fluffy seed-pods at the mercy of a fickle wind.

'Where are they going?' Holly asked as two teen-agers walked sedately past where she, Marcy and Daniel had at last found a moment to sit down in the living-room. She smiled as she heard the thunder of young feet breaking into a run once they were out of sight.

'To the game-room,' Marcy smiled contentedly. She was slumped in a pastel side chair, a cup of Anna's frothy cream perched on her stomach. Holly had never seen anyone relax so completely, or so gratefully.

'The game-room?'

'In the basement,' Daniel explained. 'There's a ping-pong table down there, billiards, some video games . . .'

'Good lord, child,' Marcy broke in. 'How could you live here this long without knowing about the game-room? It's a virtual paradise for children—and some grown-ups.' She winked at Daniel.

Holly directed a measured glance Daniel's way. 'My employer keeps me locked in the library for all my waking hours. There's no time for play when you work for Daniel Chesterfield, I'm afraid. Tell me, Marcy, which house do you live in? Perhaps I could walk over for a visit some day . . .'

'Which house?' Marcy laughed out loud. 'Oh, lord, such flattery! You think I come from around here?'

'You mean you don't?' Holly asked uncertainly.

'Oh, my, no! I'd love to have you for a visit, dear, but I think the walk would be too much for you—about thirty miles, actually, back to the heart of the city where the buildings are jammed up against each other and gardens are just a dream. That's where we all come from. Didn't you see the school bus in the driveway? That's how we got here, you know.'

'But . . I thought these were just neighbourhood children . . .'

'City children,' Marcy corrected her with a quiet smile. 'Inner city, most of them. That's why coming here every year is such a treat. Oh, Jimmy . . .' She snatched at the arm of a young boy as he hustled past. 'Gather the others now, will you? It's time we were leaving.'

Redressing twenty children of varying ages and sizes, fitting right boots and caps and coats to the right bodies, was as much confusion as Holly had

ever encountered, and twice as much fun. With the
accompanying clamour as a cover, she managed to
corner Daniel and whisper discreetly, 'Who *are*
these children? How do you know them?'

'They're friends of ours,' Daniel said absently,
smiling at the antics of two six-year-olds trying to
dress one another.

'But they've come so far . . .'

Daniel looked down at her, grinning. 'I know.
It's nice, isn't it?

'Well?' She wore a fixed smile for the benefit of
the others, but her tone was insistent. 'Aren't you
going to give them something for their trouble?'

His smile faded and he turned his head slowly to
look down at her. 'Give them something? Like
what?'

She flapped her arms. '*I* don't know. Little
presents, maybe—money—*something*. It's
Christmas, after all, and *look* at them. There isn't
one of them that couldn't use a new
coat . . .'

'Shut up, Holly.' He said it under his breath,
through his teeth, behind the cover of a false smile,
but the colour and flash of his eyes told her how
furious he really was.

'Dammit, Daniel!' she hissed through her own
teeth. 'What kind of a man are you? You just take
what you want, and never give anything in return!
You're not human at all, are you? More like some
conscienceless animal . . .'

'Holly . . .' His voice quivered dangerously, but
she ignored the warning.

'It's only money, Daniel!' she snapped contemptuously. 'You've got buckets of it! Couldn't you part with just a little, just this once? And if you don't, I will! I'll give them some of my own!'

His hand snaked out and grabbed her upper arm in a bruising grip, and still he continued to smile, making what was happening between them all the more horrible. 'Don't you dare,' he said menacingly. He jerked her arm once, violently, and in a last aside before rejoining the others, he growled, 'We'll talk after they've gone. Until then, keep your damn money to yourself.'

'Ah, Daniel!' Marcy met him half-way as he walked over, flung plump arms around his neck and smacked a kiss noisily on his cheek. 'Show the poor girl the game-room, will you?' She winked at Holly. 'And bring her along, next time you visit.'

And then the noise level increased enormously as the children assaulted Anna, Daniel and Holly with equally enthusiastic goodbyes. While Anna and Daniel basked in the attention, every hug tugged at Holly's heart-strings, magnifying her guilt at letting the children leave empty-handed. Damn Daniel, anyway. He made Scrooge look like a philanthropist! No wonder Robert hadn't liked him. No wonder *nobody* liked him, except, inexplicably, these children and Marcy.

You're a bastard, Daniel Chesterfield. She shot the thought at him from flashing eyes that glared over the heads of the children. A heartless bastard, and I'll be damned if I'll spend one more minute with you than I absolutely have to to earn my keep.

When the last child waved a last goodbye from the door, Holly spun on her heel in a swirl of skirts, and without another word fled from the despicable presence of a miser to the bitter, joyless solitude of the guest-house.

She half-expected Daniel to follow her, to bang on the guest-house door and demand that they talk.

But he didn't. At least, not right away.

The little brass clock on the mantelpiece mocked her with two resonant chimes. Two o'clock in the morning, and here she sat in front of a dwindling fire, all alone in her Christmas dress, trying to muddle through the puzzle of Daniel Chesterfield.

How could he welcome the children so eagerly into his home, and then send them away without the smallest token of appreciation for the joy they had brought with them? How could he seem so warm and gracious, so genuinely likeable at times, and still be so totally without compassion?

She had been able, if not to excuse, at least to rationalise his behaviour with the old man down at the waterfront—he had been an adult, after all, partially responsible for his own state of affairs. But the children . . . well, they were just children, blameless for the circumstances in which they found themselves. Anyone's heart would go out to them—if one *had* a heart.

She jumped and spun at the sharp rap on the door, then sprang to her feet when the door opened, admitting a cold wind, the smell of snow, and Daniel.

'I saw your light.'

Holly's eyes widened slightly as his appearance set off warning bells in her mind.

He looked tired, haggard, as if he'd spent the last several hours in exhausting physical labour. He still wore his dinner-jacket, but his tie was missing, as were the top two studs of his shirt, leaving the collar askew and his throat bare. He wore no coat, in spite of the night's frigid temperatures. Instead of putting colour into his cheeks, the cold wind seemed to have drawn it all out, until his eyes were the only spots of colour in the pale wash of his face. His hair tumbled over his forehead like dark fingers rending the white of his skin.

He stepped into the guest-house, slammed the door behind him, then simply stood there, staring at her.

Shocked by his appearance, her first impulse had been to draw him over to the warmth of the fire, but then she saw the inexplicable accusation in his eyes, and the impulse died. After all, *she* was the one who should be accusing *him*. She had nothing to apologise for, nothing to regret. *She* hadn't sent needy children away empty-handed.

She lifted her chin slightly and straightened her shoulders. 'If you've come here to explain yourself, it'll just have to wait. I don't want to talk to you.'

One side of his mouth curled upward, but his eyes never wavered. 'I never explain myself, and I didn't come here to talk.'

Holly took an alarmed step backwards, then caught herself and stood her ground. Suddenly she felt like the well-bred aristocrat, properly gowned and coiffed and behaved, threatened in her manor house by the boorish behaviour of an unpredictable intruder.

She took refuge behind the chilling tones of disdain. 'If you have nothing to say, then you have no business here. If you're any kind of a gentleman, you'll leave now.'

His steps was perfectly steady as he walked to the couch between them and braced his arms on its back; it was only the look in his eyes that made her wonder if he hadn't been drinking heavily. He spoke distinctly, with a sinister pause between each word. 'I never said I was a gentleman.'

Holly caught her breath and held it.

'Besides, that wouldn't suit your image of me anyway, would it?' His tone slid into sarcasm. 'Gentlemen are supposed to be good, kind, generous souls with impeccable manners and the purest of thoughts, like your precious Robert! Well, frankly, I think I like your image of me much better—cruel, hard, self-serving—that's what you think I am, isn't it?' He took a deep breath and brought his voice under a control so rigid that the effort pulled his eyes half-closed. 'And if that's what you think I am, then that's what I'll be.'

His eyes dropped rudely to the expanse of skin above her bodice, shocking her into a gasp that lifted her breasts visibly, prompting a smile from him that frightened her. 'Very nice,' he murmured.

'Very nice, indeed.'

'You're drunk!' she said shakily, gathering her skirts with what she hoped was aloof dignity and starting to move around the couch towards her bedroom. He intercepted her with a swiftness that belied her accusation, crushing the full sleeves of her dress under his grip.

'And you're a coward.' His voice rippled with contempt as he bent over her, forcing her backward. 'Running away from what you want—from what you are—because it isn't the kind of woman *he* wanted you to be!'

For a moment his words made her pause, and her face must have reflected that, because his grip loosened slightly. It was all the encouragement she needed to spin out of his grasp and start to run away. His hands stopped her, snaking out from behind, grabbing her arms and jerking her back against his chest. 'We're not finished yet,' he growled next to her ear, and she twisted her head away and strained for release.

'We never started!' She succeeded in pulling away slightly, only to haved him circle her waist with one arm and jerk her back, forcing the breath from her lungs. Even as she struggled, she was sharply aware of his forearm pressing inward just under her ribs. That it wasn't an altogether unpleasant sensation made her more desperate than ever to escape. Suddenly she was more afraid of her own reactions than she was of his. 'Daniel, think what you're doing! This isn't like you!'

The arm around her waist released her just

enough to allow his other hand to spin her by the shoulder until she faced him. 'Of course it is.' His smile was slow and dangerous. 'This is precisely the kind of behaviour one would expect from an animal, isn't it? A man who takes what he wants and gives nothing away? That is how you described me, if I remember correctly.'

'Daniel . . .' She lifted her hands to push at his chest, but instead found them trapped between their bodies, useless.

'You just can't admit to yourself that you could want a man like me, can you?' he growled harshly, grabbing the back of her head with both hands, jamming his fingers into the coil of her hair until all the pins went flying and her hair tumbled over his hand. 'Because I'm not like Robert.' He bent his head quickly, crushed her mouth roughly under his, then pulled away to look deeply into her eyes. 'And if you do want me,' he kissed her again, so thoroughly this time that he gasped for air when he lifted his head, 'that means you never really wanted Robert at all.'

She'd been all right until he kissed her, prepared to struggle righteously against whatever violation he attempted, as if he were a stranger accosting her on the street. But then he *had* kissed her, and whatever good intentions her mind had had were drowning the fiery, uncontrollable response of her senses.

His hands were part of her hair now, irreparably tangled in the strands, pulling her head slightly backwards, exposing her throat. His eyes were a richer, more vibrant blue than she had ever seen them. His lips moved in the blurred vision of her unblinking eyes, forming words she barely heard, and never bothered to assimilate.

'It was a fairy-tale,' he whispered hoarsely. 'What you had with Robert was nothing but a fairy-tale, but this . . .' he shifted his hands to cradle her face, pulling the tangle of her hair with them '. . . is real.'

'Daniel!' she gasped weakly, but he covered her mouth with his and trapped the breath and the words inside until she thought she would explode from the pressure. Her heart raged against her ribs as his lips and tongue moved with delicate, maddening slowness, playing her, taunting her, tempting her with sensations that blocked thought, as if someone had slammed a door on her mind. She felt his breath bursting again and again against her cheek in ragged, forceful syncopation that somehow seemed to initiate the beating of a hundred new hearts, scattered throughout her body.

The heat, this delicious, mindless heat roaring upwards from a furnace somewhere deep in her body forced her lips apart beneath his, and he shuddered, then moaned into her mouth as tongue met tongue and the breath and the spirit of two bodies mingled.

She cried out softly, involuntarily, when his lips left hers, as if he had pulled the sound from her throat simply by moving away. His hands jerked to her shoulders, holding her still, and her eyes fluttered open to find his narrowed, burning with the hot blue intensity of a gas flame. His hands pushed her arms tightly against her body, and his thumbs grazed the sides of her swollen breasts. At the moment that her head fell back languorously and her lips parted, she heard the rumble of an agonised groan that sounded like it had been ripped from the depths of his being, and she knew that he was beyond control now, and that somehow, miraculously, she had done that to him.

He dropped his arms to his sides and took a step backward, breathing through his mouth, his chin sagging to his chest, looking up at her through lowered lids. Although she sensed the trembling rise and fall of her breasts, felt the constriction of the bodice of her dress, marvelled at how the caress of silk could suddenly be so abrasive, she saw only his eyes.

'Look at you,' he gasped softly, lifting one hand, connecting their bodies only with the touch of one finger. He traced a feathery line from her jaw to her throat, down to the soft swells of white skin rising to meet his hand, and for Holly, she existed only where he touched her.

Their eyes joined by an invisible, unbreakable thread, their breathing quickened in a frantic duet that fed on its own excitement. With her senses heightened to an exquisitely painful awareness, Holly gasped helplessly when his finger reached the juncture of silk and skin, slid beneath it to scribe a line of fire over the peak of one breast. Frantically, his breath coming in hoarse gasps, he fumbled with her top button, then the second, then the

third, until her breasts tumbled gloriously free
under his gaze, quivered under the quick, rough
cupping of his callused hand, then hardened at the
startling, hungry pressure of mouth and tongue.
She felt an explosion of fire in her belly as his
mouth drew rivers of molten life upwards, shaming
the fire in the hearth with a heat that could not be
equalled. With a volition of their own, her hands
found his head and buried themselves in the coarse
silkiness of his hair.

'You will be the mistress of Chesterfield house,'
he groaned against her skin, lifting his head to let
her see in his eyes the intent she felt in his mouth
and his hands. 'Only you'll be mine—not his.'

There was a sudden, stricken cry building in her
throat, forcing her eyes wide in dismay, furiously
demanding release, but no breath passed her lips.
When the stunning, crushing blow of realisation
settled its heavy weight into her thoughts, trickles
of cold seemed to follow gravity downward,
leaving in its wake a dead chill so real that it made
her shiver.

Nothing had changed. Love had nothing to do
with what had just happened between them. Hate
was still the catalyst, and she was still simply the
spoils of an ancient, bitter contest between feuding
brothers. '. . . you'll be mine—not his.' The words
echoed and re-echoed in her mind, tormenting her,
shaming her, weakening her until she sagged in his
arms, her head falling forward against his chest,
because she didn't yet have the strength to stand on
her own.

The chill touched Daniel like the dread presence of death, tapping its bony finger on his shoulder, making him afraid. 'Holly?' he whispered, pushing her gently away to peer into her eyes, jerking his head up in surprise when she suddenly flung herself from him, clutching at the front of her dress.

'I must be the slowest learner in the world!' she shouted, reaching for a rage that would cover the strangling grip of dismay that was tearing her apart. Her hair lay in wild tangles over her bare shoulders, framing the pallor of her face, enhancing the sheer desperation of her eyes. 'You keep demonstrating so clearly that there is no love in you, no heart, and like an idiot I keep looking for one! You're damn right you're not like Robert. At least he had the courage to try to love! Your hatred keeps you from doing even that much!'

She was breathing hard now, but from the heat of anger, not passion. She lowered her head and delivered her final volley, instinctively exchanging hurt for hurt.

'You'll never touch what Robert and I shared. You'll never destroy it. You lose.' She lifted her chin and glared at him. 'To a dead man.'

She watched the colour drain from his face, but for some reason there was no satisfaction in it. He seemed altered somehow—lifeless; like a cold, marble likeness of a cruelly handsome man. And she imagined she heard the resounding clang of an iron door somewhere slamming irrevocably closed.

Stiffly, and without a word, he turned away, walked to the guest-house door, and disappeared into a night as cold as the fist clenched around her heart.

CHAPTER ELEVEN

HOLLY wakened to a frightful emptiness where her heart should have been, a feeling of loss so overwhelming that she could compare it only to the grief she had felt when Robert had died.

Her face was wet with tears she had apparently shed while she slept, and yet she couldn't remember a dream, only a lack of dreaming.

She rubbed furiously at her face, sat up in the guest-house bed, and listened to the oppressive silence. It was Monday. Daniel and Anna would disappear again by mid-morning, and the silence would be with her all day.

Suddenly the prospect of a day of complete solitude was intolerable, and she jumped from her bed and scrambled for her clothes, desperate to see a human face for only a moment, even if it were Anna's. She would be in the kitchen at this hour, cleaning up after Daniel's breakfast, preparing ahead whatever she would serve as a late supper when they returned from wherever it was they went on Mondays.

The thought that she might run into Daniel as well made her freeze for a moment, stopping the reach of her hand for her robe. But then she heard the muted roar of Daniel's sports car from outside, and nearly crumpled with relief, frowning a little as the sound of the engine became more distant and the feeling of relief changed into something else.

It's just as well that he's gone, she told herself firmly, dressing quickly, brushing her hair, touching her lashes with mascara and her lips with gloss. Facing a work day with Daniel would have been intolerable, bringing things to a head without a moment to buffer the dreadful finality of what had to be done. And a great deal remained to be done.

As much as she dreaded the intrusion on their privacy, not to mention the gentle questioning that would surely follow her request, she had to approach Hampton and Jeanine about living with them until her brownstone was finished. After last night, there was absolutely no possibility of continuing on here, either as employee or house-guest. The prospect of leaving almost made her physically ill, it was so devastating—she kept telling herself that it was the only the book she would miss.

She glanced into the dresser mirror after pulling on her boots and slipping into her cape, and noticed for the first time that she had unconsciously dressed in the garb of mourning. Long black skirt, black sweater, even a black wool band holding back the curly mass of brown hair. Her reflection gave her pause. She'd never liked herself in black, thinking the contrast with her fair skin too startling, but somehow the look seemed appropriate today.

Anna looked up sharply as she entered the

kitchen.

'He's not here,' she snapped, 'and I suspect you had something to do with that!'

For once, the old woman's open hostility did not intimidate her. Holly shrugged out of her cape, draped it carelessly over a chair, and helped herself to coffee. 'I know that. I heard his car leaving,' she said calmly, walking over and taking a seat at the table. 'So why are you still here? You usually go with him on Mondays.'

Anna snorted and turned back to the cutting board, attacking the vegetables she was slicing with a viciousness that gave new meaning to the task. 'I'll drive myself later,' she grumbled. 'What the hell did you do to him, anyway?'

Holly stifled the weak laughter building in her throat. What did *she* do to *him?* She had to concentrate to achieve the proper level of frostiness in her voice. She'd be damned if she'd spend her last conversation kowtowing to the old lady who had tried so hard to make her stay here miserable. 'Well, Anna, no doubt you'll be thrilled to know that Mr Chesterfield and I have finally come to a parting of the ways. You won't have to tolerate my presence much longer. I'll be leaving just as soon as I can arrange it. In fact, I'm driving into the city today to arrange that very thing.'

'What?' Anna slammed the knife down on the cutting board and spun around, hands on hips, face flushed with a fury that Holly found absolutely astounding. The woman hated her. She should be jumping up and down with joy. 'Don't you *dare* leave this house!' she shouted. 'Don't you *dare* do that to him!'

Holly leaned back in her chair, clutching her mug of coffee, her eyes wide with confusion. 'I . . . I thought you'd be happy I was going . . .'

'The only thing that would make me happy is if you'd never come at all! Why in God's name he hired you is beyond me! And he wasn't going to! He told Hampton that when he first recommended you, but Hampton insisted that he interview you before he decided, and after that night . . .' She shook her head violently in furious exasperation. 'I *told* him you'd be nothing but trouble! I *told* him there was no place in this house for a woman of Robert's, but he wouldn't listen!'

She turned away quickly, bracing her hands on the counter, dropping her greying head, eyes closed.

'God,' she moaned, shaking her head, 'it'll never be over. He'll never stop taking things away from him. He's been dead for a year, and still he can reach out from the grave and snatch things away . . .'

'Anna?' Holly whispered, leaning forward across the table, her eyes watchful, her voice tense. 'Anna, you have to tell me what you're talking about. I have to know why Daniel hated him. I have a right to know!'

'You don't have any rights in this house, and I don't have to tell you a thing! As a matter of fact, I've been ordered not to!'

Holly's gaze fixed on her intently. 'Ordered

not to . . . by Daniel?'

Suddenly, as Holly watched, Anna's expression altered subtly, shifting from outright fury to something almost like cunning. 'But I think I will,' she said with malevolent satisfaction. 'I think I will tell you the truth about your "dear, kind" Robert. Daniel should have told you himself, right in the beginning.'

Something sick and ugly in the old woman's smile made Holly want to jump and run from the room before it was too late, before she heard what Anna had to say; but that was silly. What *could* she say, after all? It was obvious that Daniel had always been her personal favourite of the two brothers, and that was undoubtedly what clouded her own judgement. But even Anna, twisted with hatred as she was, couldn't make a simple case of sibling rivalry into anything more than it was.

'So,' Anna's smile was more disturbing than her scowl, 'you want to know why Daniel hated Robert?'

Holly nodded steadily.

'Because Robert killed their mother.'

The simple sentence detonated with the force of an explosion, creating a pressure that forced the air from Holly's lungs and closed her eyes. This is what it must feel like to be mortally wounded, she thought, feeling the life seep out of her.

For a moment she marvelled at the extraordinary sensation, certain that if she looked down she would see herself melting into what would soon be an inconsequential puddle on the floor. Her mouth had dropped open—she was quite sure of that—but otherwise she hadn't moved, hadn't even breathed.

When she could bring her eyes to focus on Anna's again, she saw the faint glitter of something that might have been glee, and forced herself to concentrate on what she was saying. She was speaking rapidly, her voice skittering over the words, as if she was afraid her audience would run away before she had a chance to finish.

'There was a car accident when the boys were teenagers. Mr Chesterfield died, the missus was left an invalid. Bed-ridden. Paralysed from the waist down. Day after day, night after night, for years, Daniel cared for her, read to her, played games with her, made her laugh. Shooed the nurse away whenever he could be home, and did for his mother himself. He called all the things you have to do in a sick-room "responsibilities of love", and never resented a one. He was pure joy for that lady during those years. Sometimes I think he was what kept her alive, when she might have wanted to go.'

Anna's eyes had softened as she drew herself back into the past, but suddenly they hardened again. 'Robert could hardly stand to go into her bedroom, let alone stay with her for long. He'd always hated sickness, couldn't much stand to be around helpless people; but she was his mother, for God's sake!'

She closed her eyes briefly and sighed. 'Daniel didn't leave the house more than he had to— even arranged to write his column at home so he would always be close—but one day he and I both drove into the city.' Anna's eyes turned inward and clouded, and her voice dropped to a whisper. 'It was only for an hour or two, and we never thought twice about going . . . Robert was here, after all, and he promised to stay until we got back . . . he *promised* . . . but he didn't. Sat with his mother just long enough to light a cigarette, but apparently not long enough to snuff it out. Then he left—went into the city. There was a fire. Not a big fire . . . just in her room, really. But it was big enough. And Mrs Chesterfield died.'

Holly sat perfectly still, her hands pressed to her cheeks, her eyes streaming. It never occured to her to ask why Robert had done such a thing. The truth about the man she thought she had loved had been creeping into her mind and her heart gradually over the past weeks, and the horror Anna had just relayed was not so much a shock as it was a simple confirmation of what she had already begun to believe. She'd been so stupid not to have seen it before. There was so clearly something wrong, something missing in a person who never saw sadness in the world, because the sadness was always there—Robert had just refused to look at it. And if you don't look at it, if you don't acknowledge its existence, you can't change it.

So she wasn't crying for the memory of Robert she had lost; it seemed that that had been fading with every new day she spent with Daniel. Perhaps deep inside, intuitively, she had known from the beginning that, if Daniel hated, it was only because it was deserved. So now she cried for Daniel, and for the beautiful woman who watched over them both every time they stepped through the library door.

Her throat was so constricted, she could barely choke out the words. 'Anna, I'm sorry . . . you must have loved her, too . . . I'm so sorry . . .'

Anna looked at her fully for the first time in several minutes, and her brows twitched uncertainly. 'Yes, I loved her. And my husband.'

Holly blinked at her, rubbing at her eyes. 'Your husband?'

Anna nodded slowly as her own old eyes filled and ran over. 'We both worked for the Chesterfields, ever since the boys were babies. John was the gardener. He died that day, too—trying to save the missus.'

It had been the hostility that had made Anna such a formidable opponent all this time; the hatred of Robert she had transferred to Holly. Without it, she seemed to crumple in on herself, becoming visually what she was in reality—a tired old woman, with only the strength of her spirit and loyalty to Daniel supporting her. Something robbed her of that hatred now, and she suddenly looked like an empty, ravaged shell of a woman, struggling to remain erect in a stiff breeze. Clearly, she struggled, her lined face tracked with tears, her stern lips quivering with emotion; and remarkably, she succeeded. When she finally spoke again, her voice was steady. 'He'll be wondering where I am,' she said brusquely, untying her apron and dropping it uncharacteristically to the spotless floor. 'I have to go.'

And, before Holly could say a single word of protest, she found herself alone in the kitchen, mascara streaking her cheeks, remorse crushing her under the weight of complete understanding.

CHAPTER TWELVE

HOLLY drove her little car with as much reckless speed as the traffic and the snowy streets would allow. She was frantic to keep the big car Anna drove within sight, but the old woman was proving to be every bit as single-minded behind the wheel as she was in her own kitchen. Twice already, Holly had almost lost her: once on the bridge, when the bulk of a moving van had blocked her vision, and then again when they'd turned on to this highway, and she had just barely cleared the intersection before the light turned red.

Anna was far ahead of her now, negotiating the slick roadway with a skill that made Holly shake her head with grudging admiration, but it didn't matter if she lost her now. She knew exactly where she was going.

She parked at the far edge of the car park, butting the nose of her little car up against a bank of ploughed snow, then got out, tugged her cape more closely around her, and turned to look at the old brick edifice lumbering across the bleak landscape. Block letters a foot high were carved into a concrete slab over the front entrance. 'Children's Memorial Hospital'.

So this was where Daniel spent every Monday—

and Anna, too. A rather sad smile touched her lips as she pulled her hood up against the frigid wind and began the long walk across the car park.

Damn you, Daniel, you should have told me about the fire. The thought beat like a drum in her head, marking the time of her boots crunching in the snow. All this time I had Robert up on a pedestal, and you the villain at his feet, just because you hated him. Dammit, you should have told me. I didn't understand.

She bent her head against the wind and jammed her hands into the pockets of her cape, wondering absently why she had come here, and what good it would do. Daniel's hatred for his dead brother hadn't lessened just because she understood the reason for it, and if there was one thing Holly was sure of, it was that there wasn't room in her life for hatred. There wasn't time for it, either. Robert had taught her that much.

She smiled at a sudden flash of memory— Robert, standing in front of that department store, spreading a warm glow among complete strangers with a simple word, a gesture, a smile. That was what she had loved, really—not Robert, because she had never really known Robert; it was the *idea* of Robert that had captured her heart. The idea of one person being able to make a difference, being able to see joy where no one else could, and share it with anyone who happened to pass by.

Perhaps Daniel was right—perhaps she had been in love with a fairy-tale, an image of a man with no substance, as elusive as a mirage that pictured only what one wished to see, instead of what really was. The reality was that Robert had been criminally irresponsible, as deceptively shallow as a reflecting pool, but the reflection *had* been beautiful. The image, if not the man, had been worthy of love. But Daniel would never be able to understand that. He'd been so determined to be unlike the brother he hated that he had become the antithesis—a dark, bitter man incapable of joy, and incapable of love—as incomplete in one way as his brother had been in another.

She touched the hood of Anna's car as she walked past it. The steady ticking of the cooling engine marked the sad beat of a heart that wished desperately that things could have been different.

'I'm looking for Daniel Chesterfield,' she told the nurse at the huge, horseshoe-shaped front desk.

The girl cocked her head with a peculiar smile, as if the question had been ridiculous. 'He's in the Chesterfield Wing, of course.'

'The Chesterfield Wing?' Holly echoed weakly.

The girl nodded with a forgiving smile, suddenly understanding that this particular visitor wasn't familiar with the hospital. 'Sorry. Danny's been supporting it for so long, and he's here so often, that we all call Children's Therapy the Chesterfield Wing. Third floor, turn right when you get out of the lift.'

'Thank you.' Holly smiled weakly, as much surprised to learn Daniel supported an entire wing of a hospital as she was to hear him called 'Danny'.

The third floor was as unlike a hospital as
anything Holly could imagine. White-clad nurses
and orderlies peppered the halls, but it seemed they
were constantly dodging children of all ages, some
on crutches, some in wheelchairs, all exercising
apparent freedom to roam the corridors. The walls
were covered with brightly painted cartoon murals,
all depicting hospital-gowned children in various,
fantastic forms of flight. There were winged horses
carrying children through puffy white clouds;
smiling aeroplanes and hot air balloons lifting a
cargo of smiling toddlers far above the earth; even
a gilded carriage drawn by a team of feathered
doves towards a distant rainbow. Holly followed
the walls like a story, reaching out every now and
then to touch the bright paint with a wonder that
suggested she thought the pictures would come to
life.

'Holly? Holly, is that you?'

Marcy was in the white uniform and peaked cap
of a nurse, hurrying towards her with a big smile
and an outstretched hand. 'Well!' She pumped
Holly's hand as if she hadn't seen her in years. 'He
finally brought you along for a visit. Good for
him. He could have told me, though. I didn't even
know you were here. Come on. I'll give you the
grand tour.'

Speechless, Holly allowed herself to be led down
a side corridor, into one ward, and then another,
and then another, numbed by the non-stop rattle
of Marcy's monologue. She met twenty children in
the first ten minutes, some of them horribly

scarred, some of them in casts, some of them weak from prolonged battle with one disease or another. To each one she was introduced as 'Daniel's and Anna's friend', and the phrase was like a prearranged cue word that guaranteed the flash of a trusting smile.

'So,' Marcy asked as they made their way to the nurses' lounge, 'what do you think of Daniel's children?'

'Daniel's children?' she asked weakly, sinking to a battered leather couch, gratefully accepting the styrofoam cup of coffee Marcy offered.

'Well,' Marcy chuckled, her eyes twinkling, 'I suppose we'll have to find another name for them, after you two have some of your own, although I don't know how the kids will take giving up the title. Being one of Danny's kids—lord!' She rolled her eyes. 'When I think of how we've dangled that plum over the years—"now, you have to eat, if you want to be one of Danny'd kids," or "but you *have* to go to therapy; all of Danny's kids go to therapy"—oh, what am I telling you all this for? I'm sure Daniel talks your ear off about this place, and I can't tell you how glad I am to see you want to get involved, too. I must admit we were all a little worried when he said he was getting married—afraid the new Mrs Chesterfield wouldn't think much of all the time and effort he puts into this place!' She leaned over and patted Holly's knee. 'That was before I met you, of course. I put everyone's mind at ease on that point this morning. Now, when's the grand occasion?

And don't think you can get away with sneaking off to a Justice of the Peace somewhere. We wouldn't stand for that . . . good lord, girl! You're as white as a sheet. You aren't sick, are you?'

'No . . . no . . . it's just that . . I didn't know Daniel had . . .'

'Ah!' Marcy rocked back and shook her head. 'You didn't know he'd told anybody, did you? Well, don't chide him for that. Happy secrets were never meant to be kept.' She rose to her feet and brushed at imaginary wrinkles in the front of her uniform. 'I wish I could spend more time with you, but I'd better get back to work. Come on. Daniel and Anna are in the playroom. I'll take you there.'

'Marcy?' Holly grabbed her hand at the door. 'Did you know Daniel's brother?'

Marcy's smile stiffened slightly. 'Robert? Sure. I knew him. As well as anyone knew him around here, I suppose. He never did show his face in the wards, though. Just dropped off presents at the main desk and ran as if the whole place were contagious. Damn . . .' She shook her head and sighed. 'That wasn't a very charitable thing to say, was it? And I suppose Robert's heart was in the right place—it just wasn't big enough, that's all. Not like Daniel's.'

Marcy dropped her off at a pair of glass doors that led into an enormous room cluttered with toys and books and games and the sound of laughter. Holly stood at the entrance, gazing through the glass at the man whose heart was big enough—the man she had thought incapable of giving love.

Daniel was sprawled on his stomach on the floor, reading earnestly from a picture-book propped in front of him. He wore battered jeans, a sweatshirt with toothy cartoon duck on the front, and a baseball cap turned sideways. Children were scattered around him like fallen leaves, leaning against his body, hovering over his shoulder—one youngster was even perched on his back, peering at the book over his head. It was obvious that whatever he was reading excited them. Their eyes were all saucer-like, intently following his finger as it traced across the page.

Holly's eyes shifted to a far corner of the room, barely visible through the doors, and she smiled even as she blinked hard, to keep from crying. There was Anna, huddled on the floor in her starched black dress, hunkered over a game board filled with marbles, as intent as Holly had ever seen her. She rolled a pair of dice, made a terrible face and slapped her forehead. The three children circling the game board laughed and clapped with delight.

'Aren't they something?'

Holly jumped and spun to face the nurse at her side, a pretty young brunette barely out of her teens.

'Sorry.' The girl smiled. 'It's these darn soft-soled shoes. You can sneak up on anybody, without meaning to.' She looked back through the glass door and smiled. 'Look at that imp, Todd. He's on Danny's back again.'

Holly followed her eyes to the tow-headed youngster astride Daniel, one of the few children in the room without a cast or a sling, or even a paleness that suggested illness. 'He's a beautiful child. Will he be going home soon?'

The nurse turned her head slowly towards Holly. 'No,' she said softly. 'I'm afraid not.' And it wasn't the words or the way she said them, but her expression that told Holly the beautiful, healthy-looking boy wouldn't be going home at all. Ever.

Holly's hand flew to her mouth and pressed hard, and she took a quick step backward from the door, as if she could back away from the certainty of death itself if she only moved quickly enough. She jerked her head back to stare at the deceptively happy scene beyond those doors, and it became a room of horrors that made her want to run; a hideous, monstrous place where the ticking of a clock measured the moments left to a beautiful child. This was the ugliness Robert could never bring himself to face, and for one heart-shattering moment she could empathise with that. It would be so much easier, wouldn't it, just to close your eyes and run and pretend you'd never seen, pretend the sadness didn't exist? Give the beggar money so he'd go away—so you didn't have to listen to his tale of woe, so you didn't have to know the misery that was his life. Leave the presents on the desk, but never, never visit the children, so you didn't have to feel their pain. And greet the stranger and smile and wish him Merry Christmas, but then for God's sake turn away, quickly, before he got too close . . .

'But that isn't really giving, is it?' Holly

whispered, her lips close to the glass, her eyes spilling over as she watched Daniel grinning into the story-book and Todd patting him happily on the head.

'I beg your pardon?' The nurse was watching her carefully, her brows tipped with concern.

'Nothing.' Holly smiled through her tears, then reached out impulsively and patted the nurse on her shoulder. 'Nothing at all.'

'Did you want to go in?'

Holly shook her head. 'No. Not this time. But I'll be back.'

CHAPTER THIRTEEN

HOLLY was waiting for them in the kitchen of the main house when they came in through the back door. Anna took one look at Holly, standing at *her* stove, wearing *her* apron, stirring something in one of *her* pans, and snapped to a halt so fast that Daniel ran into her back.

'Just what do you think you're doing?'

'Making supper, that's what.' Holly dipped a spoon into the hot chilli, tasted it gingerly, then nodded with satisfaction. She glanced at Anna, then turned quickly back to the stove to avoid looking at Daniel. 'Stop holding your breath, Anna,' she said calmly. 'You look as if you're about to explode. I didn't lay waste to your kitchen, and I'm not making hemlock, so take off your coats, both of you, and go sit down so we can eat.'

'I think I'll just run upstairs and change first . . .'

'Don't bother, Daniel.' Holly turned and looked at him directly for the first time. 'I've already seen the duck. And the baseball cap you've got jammed in your pocket.'

Daniel looked at her steadily, never moving, while Anna bustled around him, making exasperated noises as she shrugged out of her coat.

'You were at the hospital,' he said quietly, still looking at her.

Holly nodded.

'I didn't see you there.'

'I saw you. Why didn't you tell me that was what you did on Mondays?'

He smiled for the first time. 'You never asked.'

All of Holly's smugness evaporated instantly, and she just stood there in Anna's spattered apron, her mouth slightly open, her expression a perfect study of dismay. He was right. She had never asked. Where do you go on Mondays, Daniel? Do you have a favourite charity? What do you care about? If she'd just asked any of those questions, she would have known from the beginning what kind of man Daniel really was. But because his generosity wasn't as visible as Robert's, as *superficial,* she reminded herself, she had assumed he didn't have any. Oh, Daniel, she mourned silently. Has it always been like that for you? Has your goodness always gone unnoticed next to Robert's flamboyance?

'Chilli's hot,' she said hoarsely, turning away quickly, grabbing for a stack of dishes.'

'I'll do that,' Anna snapped, snatching them out of her hands. And then, while Daniel was out of earshot hanging up his coat, she hissed furiously into Holly's ear, 'God forbid you should have to serve yourself your last meal here!'

Holly looked at her, blinked once, then smiled
. . . wickedly, she hoped. 'You'd better get used to
me, Anna,' she hissed back, 'because I'm going to
be around for a long time. You're going to have
to outlive me to get this place to yourself
again.

Anna jerked her head back on her shoulders,
glared at her, and then grunted. If Holly hadn't
been looking very, very closely, she might have
missed the little twitch that marked a smile nipped
in the bud.

'Chilli,' she grumbled, ladling an enormous
amount into a bowl. 'I hate chilli. Always have,
always will. Besides, I'm too tired to eat. I'll just
take this to my room, in case I get desperate
later.'

'Anna?'

The old woman turned at the doorway. 'What is
it, Holly?'

It was the first time she'd ever called her by
name.

'Stay,' Holly said softly. 'Eat with us.'

There was silence between the two women for a
moment as their eyes linked across the room.
'Another time,' she said finally, pushing
through the door, and the words were like a
promise.

'What's with you two?' Daniel asked quietly,
coming up behind her. 'For a moment there, you
were almost civil to each other,'

Holly turned around and found herself looking

directly into the garish blue eyes of the silly smiling duck on his sweatshirt. 'I don't know if I can talk seriously to a man wearing a duck.'

His smile was pained, as if someone had pulled up strings attached to the corners of his mouth. 'It's my favourite outfit.'

'I believe it.'

Blue eyes searched brown, for just a moment, then he turned away from her and went to the refrigerator. 'Beer OK?' He hefted two frosty bottles. 'I think we're fresh out of a wine vintage that goes with chilli.'

'Careful, Daniel,' she smiled. 'That was perilously close to a joke. Humour is a very human characteristic, you know.'

His head jerked towards her, spilling a tangle of black curls across his forehead. 'I've never denied being human. You were the one who labelled me an animal, I believe.'

'That's the only side you ever let me see.'

It took all her will-power not to turn away from his stare, not to be intimidated by the anger she saw in his eyes. He'd been holding a bottle in each hand, but now he slammed them both down on the counter, moved rapidly over to where she stood and grabbed her by the shoulders. She felt the cold of his hands through her sweater, and trembled. His fingers pressed into her flesh, demanding that she look up at him, and she did. Her hair, loose and crackling with the static of dry heat, tumbled off her shoulders and down her back. His voice coursed through her body like an electric current, felt, more than heard.

'Every minute we've spent together I've had to fight to keep my hands off you,' he growled, his eyes narrowed, his mouth a breath away from hers. 'And that's been just too earthy a response for you, hasn't it? A little too far removed—too far *below*—the way Robert behaved. If that makes me an animal, then so be it. I don't give a damn!'

He jerked her against him so savagely that it forced the breath from her lungs to explode softly against his face. He covered her mouth quickly, frantically, as if to capture the last vestiges of her breath before it could escape, and when her lips parted eagerly beneath his, he pushed her away, gasping, his eyes wide.

'What the hell is this?'

She felt a shudder pass through his hands into her body.

'Sudden surrender? Just because I spend Mondays in a kids' hospital? Just because that makes me a little like your precious Robert?'

He shoved her from him so violently that she had to take a quick step backward to keep from falling. She dropped her chin and looked up at him through lowered lids, feeling the heat of anger rise to her eyes and collect there in a brown fire. She had expected anything except a callous rejection, and her reaction was swift and mindless. He had expected anything except fury, and a certain wariness crept into his expression.

'You *always* throw Robert's name up between us!' she hissed. 'Like some magic shield to protect you!'

Now *he* took a quick, flabbergasted step backward, his eyes flashing denial.

'It's true!' She moved towards him, following the furious trail her eyes blazed. 'You're so damn determined to be as different from Robert as you can be that you lock up every decent emotion you feel—hide it from the world so that no one knows you *do* feel—because that would make you like him. And it's senseless! You're not a *bit* like Robert! You're what Robert wanted to be, and never could!'

She stood mere inches from him, breathing hard, her face tilted stubbornly upward in a challenge, her nostrils flaring.

His face quieted slowly, like a home movie unreeling one frame at a time, and when the transition was complete his eyes broke her heart. In them she saw the reflections of old sorrows, pain too heavy to be borne, but borne, none the less; a desperate, vast loneliness that made one think of endless stretches of desert instead of just an empty room; and worst of all, a poignant longing that had never found voice. She had never seen this Daniel Chesterfield. She wondered if anyone had. He didn't have to tell her what it had cost him to let her see it.

She lifted her right hand and laid it against his cheek. He winced slightly, but simply squeezed his eyes shut and remained still, as if to demonstrate that he could bear any pain she chose to inflict. The moment was unbearably full, and somehow Holly knew that however their bodies would join in the future, they would never again experience the closeness of spirit that linked them now, through the simple touch of her hand on his cheek.

Suddenly he grabbed her hand and buried his face in her palm, his lips moving almost imperceptibly over the smooth skin. Black strands of his hair danced over her white fingers as she let them drift slowly over the brow she had never touched before.

'What do you feel, Daniel?' she whispered. 'What do you feel for me?'

He lifted his head, then his body followed as he straightened to his full height and looked down at her. 'Too much.' His voice was hoarse, dry. 'I feel too much. I don't know what to do with this much feeling. I never did.'

Holly felt a catch in her throat that trapped her words, holding them momentarily captive somewhere close to her heart. Perhaps it was the one thing of value Robert had taught her; the one thing that still glittered brightly in the murky legacy of a man who had only been a fairy-tale. 'You know what to do, Daniel,' she whispered, her fingers trembling on the roughness of his cheek. 'You've always known what to do with feelings that big. You pass them on.'

And then she smiled into his eyes because she saw the passion flaring there, the desire, but it was distant, pushed back for a moment to make room for something else, something bigger.

'Oh, good grief!' Anna snapped from the doorway, her expression considerably less stern than the tone of her voice. 'A decent woman can't even walk into her own kitchen around here!'

Holly backed away from Daniel with the flustered expression of an embarrassed schoolgirl, but Daniel just smiled, then leaned back against the counter, resting on an elbow, the fingers of his hand flexing towards the floor. His lips were quirked in a dark, playfully menacing smile, and his eyes remained fastened on Holly's, saying absolutely unspeakable things that made the colour rise in her face as rapidly as if they'd been uttered aloud. She wanted to command him to stop looking at her like that, to tell him that anyone would know precisely what was going through his mind with one quick glance at his face—but she didn't trust her voice. So she just stood there like a mute, wide-eyed simpleton as he walked towards her, took her arm, and led her gently, solicitously, silently, out of the back door, and through the shovelled path towards the guest-house.

They'd forgotten their coats, but neither one of them felt the cold.

Anna stared at the door that had just closed behind them, sighed, and then whispered so softly that she barely heard her own voice, 'Merry Christmas—to both of you.'

Then she turned back to chilli pot and started

scooping another ladleful into her empty bowl. It
hadn't been bad, actually.

CHAPTER FOURTEEN

DANIEL slammed the guest-house door closed behind them, led Holly to the couch that faced the fireplace, then pushed her down unceremoniously. 'There are a few things we have to get straight,' he told her firmly.

'You bet there are,' she came back quickly. 'Marcy tells me we're going to get married.'

He slammed his mouth closed.

'Well?' She raised her eyebrows. 'Care to tell an interested bystander when you decided that?'

He shrugged nonchalantly. 'A while back.'

'A while back,' she repeated, her lips pursed. 'I see. Do you announce to the world that you're going to marry every woman you want to take to bed, or can I assume that you're at least a little fond of me as well?'

'Fond of you?' He gasped weakly, as if she'd punched him in the stomach, then covered his lapse by shouting, 'Fond of you? Are you crazy? I'm in love with you? I have been, since that first night!'

Holly watched with wide eyes as he turned, shoved up the sleeves of his sweatshirt, and crouched at the hearth. The muscles in his forearms flexed, then stretched as he banged heavy logs angrily on the grate, then snapped a match to the kindling beneath. He spun on the balls of his feet without rising, his arms resting on his knees, his eyes intent.

'We'll talk about that later,' he said brusquely, as if love and marriage were only things of minor importance. 'I'll ask, and you can answer, and we'll do it all according to the rules, but not until I tell you a few things.'

'Daniel . . .'

'Don't say anything, Holly. Not yet. Not until I have a chance to explain myself.'

'But that's just it, Daniel. You don't have to . . .'

He scowled her into silence. 'I told you I'd explain why we didn't give anything to the carollers. You never gave me the chance.'

'It doesn't matter, Daniel . . .'

'Be quiet. I want you to know.' He turned to watch the fire catch as he talked. 'Those kids are our graduates—the ones who've made it out of the physical therapy ward—and ones who've learned all over again to walk, or talk, or do whatever it was they couldn't do before. They've all come back from critical illness or injury. They've all fought long and hard to go home again. Anna and I watch them fight, help them when we can, give them whatever we're capable of giving. And then, when they're able, they want to give something back. So they come and sing for us at Christmas. It's the only gift most of them can give. If we gave them something in return, it wouldn't be a gift any more, it would only be a trade.' He turned his head and and looked at her, his eyes softly vulnerable. 'Everybody needs to give, Holly,' he said softly. 'I wouldn't deprive them of that pleasure for anything.'

She just stared at him, not knowing what to say.

He frowned, then turned back to poke at the fire. 'And the tramp on the waterfront . . . he's not just any tramp. That's Johnny Markerson.' He closed his eyes and shook his head, as if confronted with the vision of a personal failure. 'He's been in and out of alcohol treatment so often, they've put a revolving door in for him at the clinic. You give that man drink money and he falls into the ocean. Without it, he sobers up eventually, goes back to work at the restaurant, and gives his wife a few days' peace. They lost their son a few years back. Johnny's still having trouble with that.'

How could he know all that? Holly wondered. How could he know so much about a tramp on the street? Because he cared enough to find out, she told herself, closing her eyes, smiling ruefully as she saw a picture of Robert, giving, always giving, to anyone who asked—giving money, gifts, cheer—anything, except pieces of himself.

She sighed noisily and leaned forward, meeting his eyes. 'Are you finished explaining yourself?'

'I just wanted you to know . . . before we talked about anything else . . . I'm not a monster, Holly.'

She looked down and plucked a loose thread from the couch cushion. 'I never said you were a monster. I said you were an animal.' She lifted her eyes expectantly. 'Of course, there you are, just as civilised as you can be, and here I am, relatively untouched . . .' She shrugged at the distance between them. 'I could have been wrong.'

He looked at her for a long time, then pushed his hands against his knees and rose to his feet. 'I can't give you what Robert gave you,' he said carefully.

'No,' she whispered, 'you can give me more . . .'

The firelight danced behind him as he walked slowly towards her, so slowly that it took him endless years to cross the space that kept them apart, and the wait was bearable only because she saw the promise in his eyes. She caught her breath as she saw for the very first time a family resemblance between the brothers, for there, in Daniel's eyes, she saw the same spiritual radiance she had seen in Robert's so often; but there was something more—a deeper, more intense fire that crackled with the passion of a man for a woman—the kind of passion that would bring that radiance down to earth and make it human.

And oh, my, she thought, tipping her head back and closing her eyes as his mouth found her neck and his hands slipped under her sweater, being merely human was the most magnificent thing.

Harlequin Presents

Coming Next Month

1231 THAT SPECIAL TOUCH Anne Beaumont
Elisa enjoys her summer sketching tourists in Corfu, which makes a good refuge from her problems back home. Now it seems that Rafe Sinclair and his daughter, Penny, are about to present her with equally challenging ones here

1232 THE FALCON'S MISTRESS Emma Darcy
Bethany runs afoul of autocratic Prince Zakr, ruler of Bayrar, almost as soon as her plane lands. He thinks he can bend her to his will as easily as he trains his hunting falcons. But Bethany has plans of her own.

1233 LOVE'S REWARD Robyn Donald
Jake Ferrars has an overwhelming impact on women, as Cathy Durrant has on men. Two beautiful people, each one knowing about the other But how can they possibly believe that the rumors they've heard about each other are true?

1234 AWAKENING DREAMS Vanessa Grant
They are lucky to be alive—but trekking out of the wilderness with Jesse Campbell is not Crystal's idea of normal travel, especially for a city tax auditor But a quick assessment of their situation shows they have no alternative

1235 TODAY, TOMORROW AND FOREVER Sally Heywood
Inheriting part ownership of a Mediterranean island is such a thrill that Shanna wants to see it right away. Meeting Paul Elliott on the way is a bonus, until Shanna realizes that he's keeping a secret from her

1236 SEDUCTIVE STRANGER Charlotte Lamb
Returning to England after ten years, Prue wants to see her father again and to find out the truth about the past. She doesn't welcome interference from Josh Killane—he makes her temper soar and her heart beat faster!

1237 STRANGE ENCOUNTER Sally Wentworth
Kelly Baxter, after her parents' death, tracks down lost relatives in England. She can't help wondering, though, when she does discover a long-lost cousin in the Cotswolds, why Byron Thorne is most reluctant to let them meet.

1238 TEMPORARY BRIDE Patricia Wilson
Charlotte can't let her beloved uncle go to prison, even if he did commit fraud. Kit Landor says he won't prosecute if she will marry him. With no other alternative, Charlotte agrees—but doesn't intend to let him have it all his own way…

Available in January wherever paperback books are sold, or through Harlequin Reader Service:

In the U.S.
901 Fuhrmann Blvd.
P.O. Box 1397
Buffalo, N.Y 14240-1397

In Canada
P.O. Box 603
Fort Erie, Ontario
L2A 5X3

CHRISTMAS IS FOR KIDS

Spend this holiday season with nine very special children. Children whose wishes come true at the magical time of Christmas.

Read American Romance's CHRISTMAS IS FOR KIDS— heartwarming holiday stories in which children bring together four couples who fall in love. Meet:

Frank, Dorcas, Kathy, Candy and Nicky—They become friends at St. Christopher's orphanage, but they really want to be adopted and become part of a real family, in #321 *A Carol Christmas* by Muriel Jensen.

Patty—She's a ten-year-old certified genius, but she wants what every little girl wishes for: a daddy of her own, in #322 *Mrs. Scrooge* by Barbara Bretton.

Amy and Flash—Their mom is about to deliver their newest sibling any day, but Christmas just isn't the same now—not without their dad. More than anything they want their family reunited for Christmas, in #323 *Dear Santa* by Margaret St. George.

Spencer—Living with his dad and grandpa in an all-male household has its advantages, but Spence wants Santa to bring him a mommy to love, in #324 *The Best Gift of All* by Andrea Davidson.

These children will win your hearts as they entice—and matchmake—the adults into a true romance. This holiday, invite them—and the four couples they bring together—into your home.

Look for all four CHRISTMAS IS FOR KIDS books available now from Harlequin American Romance. And happy holidays!

XMAS-KIDS-1R

Wonderful, luxurious gifts can be yours with proofs-of-purchase from any specially marked "Indulge A Little" Harlequin or Silhouette book with the Offer Certificate properly completed, plus a check or money order (do not send cash) to cover postage and handling payable to Harlequin/Silhouette "Indulge A Little, Give A Lot" Offer. We will send you the specified gift.

Mail-in-Offer

OFFER CERTIFICATE

Item:	A. Collector's Doll	B. Soaps in a Basket	C. Potpourri Sachet	D. Scented Hangers
# of Proofs-of-Purchase	18	12	6	4
Postage & Handling	$3.25	$2.75	$2.25	$2.00
Check One				

Name _____

Address _____ Apt. # _____

City _____ State _____ Zip _____

ONE PROOF OF PURCHASE

To collect your free gift by mail you must include the necessary number of proofs-of-purchase plus postage and handling with offer certificate.

GIVE A LOT

HP-3

Harlequin®/Silhouette®

Mail this certificate, designated number of proofs-of-purchase and check or money order for postage and handling to:

INDULGE A LITTLE
P.O. Box 9055
Buffalo, N.Y. 14269-9055